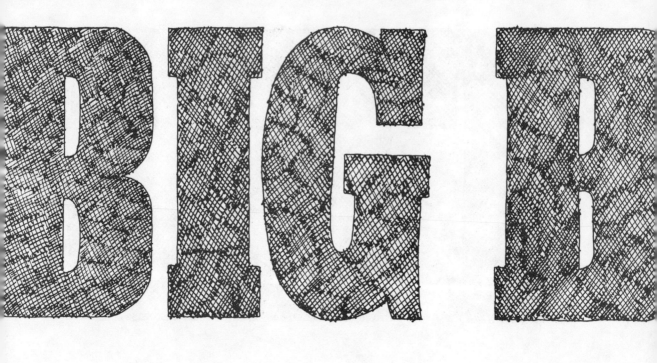

BIG B

Psittacosaurus

A BROWN PAPER SCHOOL BOOK

The Big Beast Book
Dinosaurs and How They Got That Way

by
Jerry Booth

Drawings by Martha Weston

Little, Brown and Company
Boston   Toronto

A YOLLA BOLLY PRESS BOOK

*This Brown Paper School book was edited and prepared for publication at
The Yolla Bolly Press, Covelo, California. The series is under the super-
vision of James and Carolyn Robertson. Editorial and production staff:
Barbara Youngblood and Diana Fairbanks.*

*The photograph on page 38 is reprinted with the
permission of John H. Ostrom, Peabody Museum,
Yale University.*

FIRST EDITION

Library of Congress Cataloging-in-Publication Data

Booth, Jerry.
    The big beast book.

    (A Brown paper school book)
    Summary: An introduction to dinosaurs with
instructions for related projects.
    1. Dinosaurs—Juvenile literature.   [1. Dinosaurs]
I. Weston, Martha, ill.   II. Title.   III. Title:
Dinosaurs and how they got that way.
QE862.D5B64   1988   567.9'1   87-36206
ISBN 0-316-10263-6
ISBN 0-316-10266-0 (pbk.)

HC: 10 9 8 7 6 5 4 3 2 1
PB: 10 9 8 7 6 5 4 3 2 1

*Published simultaneously in Canada
by Little, Brown & Company (Canada) Limited*

PRINTED IN THE UNITED STATES

FOR NIKO

Many people helped me with their ideas and support, but I'd particularly like to thank Barbara Ando, Mark Goodwin, Kyoko Kishi, Ruth Sawdo, Gigi Bridges, Sue Jagoda, and Dr. Kevin Padian.

CONTENTS

Dinosaurs are a problem. That's good.

It's not that they're a problem, as in trouble. They're a problem as in puzzle, or mind stretcher.

Just as some dinosaur names exercise your tongue, learning to think about dinosaurs is a good way to exercise your mind and your imagination. That's because you'll never see one. The last dinosaur died millions of years before your quadruple-great-grandmother was born. They're very different from any animal living today. And the main way we can find out about them is by puzzling over a few bones that turned to stone. Now that's a problem!

This book won't tell you how great dinosaurs were. It'll show you ways to find out for yourself. You'll learn to measure them. You'll walk in their trackways. You'll race them mathematically. You'll ponder their colors, their teeth, and their headgear. You'll learn to identify them and sort them, and you'll learn how to explore for fossils. You'll even do some stargazing, looking for clues to why they disappeared.

After all that, you'll have to agree: dinosaurs are a problem. And that's not bad because a good problem can teach you lots of things.

CHAPTER

IS YOUR PERSPECTIVE
GEOLOGIC?

Life Before We Knew About Dinosaurs

Think how much more exciting life is now that we know about dinosaurs. Throughout history kids have been finding strange rocks that are shaped like bones, but they've never known quite what to make of them. Adults all over the world have tried to explain these mysterious rocks to puzzled kids.

But the rocks kept turning up faster than people could make up stories to explain them.

And, finally, a few people decided that the "rocks" weren't from dragons or giants or serpents at all. These people noticed that the rocks were fossils and that they looked a lot like the bones of living animals. They decided the bones were from animals that had once lived on the earth but had since disappeared.

Finally, on August 2, 1841, at a scientific meeting in Plymouth, England, paleontologist Richard Owen made a fateful announcement. He had invented a word to describe the extinct animals represented by the strangest of these fossils. The word was

Owen's new word caught on. Dinosaur means "terrible lizard" in Greek, and it captured the public's imagination. Soon all of England was engulfed in the first known case of "Dinosaurmania." Fortunately, this is a delightful disease from which we've never really recovered.

But wait. With all the excitement about dinosaurs, it's sometimes easy to forget that they were animals that breathed and ate, were born and died, just like all the other animals on the earth. Let's take a look at dinosaurs as animals, not as media stars or advertising gimmicks, and explore ways to find out more about them.

11

Stretching Out Your Sense of Time

One of the main reasons people had such a hard time discovering dinosaurs was that they had no sense of time. Well, not a good enough one anyway. If they thought about it at all, most people believed that the earth was only a few thousand years old and that it had probably been pretty much the same since the beginning.

Today, most people know in their heads that the earth is much older and that it is changing all the time. But most of us still have real problems when we try to imagine time in a geologic sense. This is because our sense of time and space are shaped by things that are familiar to us. You might think the United States has been around a long time, but it's only about 200 years old. Once you can imagine something 5,000 times older than that, you'll begin to see how geologists (scientists who study the history of the earth) and paleontologists (scientists who study ancient plants and animals) look at time.

So before you go off hunting for dinosaurs, you need to take a few minutes to readjust your sense of time, stretch it out a bit. This requires first that you understand the idea of one million. Then you'll have a better idea about where dinosaurs, as well as humans, fit into the overall scheme of things.

One in a Thousand Thousands

Can you think of anything that might be a million years old? A million years is a long time to most people. And it is an impressive number. But on a paleontologist's or geologist's time scale, it passes in the blink of an eye.

One way to think about a million years is to compare it to your own age. Here's how you can do that. First, round off your age to the nearest ten. So if you're between 5 and 14, you would round your age off to 10. If you're 15 to 24, round it off to 20. If you're 75 to 84 round it off to . . . well, you get the idea.

Now, imagine that the length of a football field (100 yards) represents a million years. How much of the field does your age cover? First, find out how many years are represented by 1 yard. To do that, divide 1,000,000 years by 100 yards. What did you get? Right, 1 yard equals 10,000 years. Can you name anything that's 10,000 years old? Probably not, so keep dividing.

Since you're down to 1 yard (or 10,000 years), you can do the rest of this activity with a yardstick. First, how many inches in a yard? Divide 10,000 years by this. What do you get? 277? Good. Let's call it 280 (remember, you're rounding off to the nearest ten).

So if 100 yards equal a million years, then anything that is 280 years old is represented by 1 inch on your yardstick. What was happening 280 years ago? Was the United States an independent nation? Had the word *dinosaur* been invented? Things have sure changed in that inch of time!

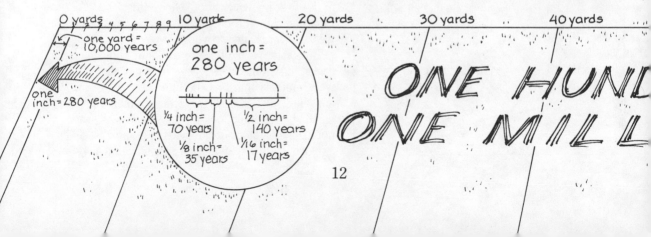

How much time is represented by ½ inch? Do you know anything or anybody that old? When we get down to ¼ inch, we're looking at about 70 years. Now, maybe you have an older relative who will fit on your scale? If we go down to ⅛ inch, someone who is 35 years old will register. How many people that age do you know?

You're probably getting the picture by now. If a 100-yard field represents a million years and you are 10 years old, then you take up approximately ¹⁄₃₂ inch on the field. In other words, you're there, but you don't take up much space.

To make you feel even smaller, consider the fact that if we used this same scale for the entire geologic history of the earth, it would cover about 4,600 football fields.

It looks like you're just a blip on the cosmic scale. But don't be sad. You might be cosmically small, but your brain can cut the millennia down to size! That's what you'll do next.

Striding Through the Millennia

Now that you've reduced yourself to a cosmic dust speck, you're going to transform yourself into a time-traveling giant who can leap back in time a million years with a single footstep. To do that, we'll make a time line that covers the entire history of our planet.

Geologists and paleontologists divide the history of the earth into four eras—the Cenozoic, the Mesozoic, the Paleozoic, and the Precambrian. The Precambrian era stretches from when the earth formed, 4.6 billion years ago, to 600 million years ago. The Paleozoic era (600 to 225 million years ago) marked the first appearance of complex animals and plants. The Mesozoic era (225 to 64 million years ago) is when the dinosaurs flourished. And, finally, the Cenozoic era (64 million years ago to the present) saw the appearance of animals and plants similar to those you see every day.

Each of these eras in turn is divided into periods, which are divided into epochs, which are divided into ages. All the terms get confusing really fast, but in order to do some time traveling in search of dinosaurs, we will need some guideposts. Let's keep things simple by dividing our time line into just ten parts. Then we'll make signs to warn other time travelers about the animals they may encounter as they pass through each part. **You will need:**

lots of room—a playground, a field, or a city block is fine
ten pieces of cardboard (about 20 inches by 30 inches) for signs
felt markers
ten sticks to hold up your signs
masking tape or tacks to attach them to the sticks

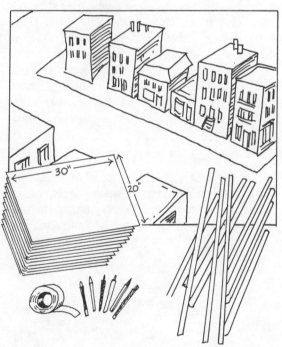

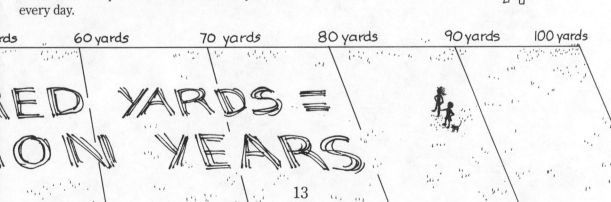

13

Our signs should look something like this: ✗ (Actually, sign number 10 is optional. Use it only if you have a little brother you'd like to send on a long hike!) Once you've made your signs, use tape or tacks to attach each sign to a stick.

You're almost ready to start walking, but first a warning. The dates you are using are estimates based on current fossil finds. The great thing about science is that it is never finished. As new fossils are found, the dates given here are apt to change. That's okay; we're still way ahead of our ancestors. After all, just 300 years ago most people were certain that the earth was only 6,000 years old.

1.

Stick the first sign in the ground at the beginning of the time line. From this point on, each step you take will represent a million years in the history of the earth. (Remember, an entire football field in the first activity represented a million years!)

2.

Take two steps and stick sign number 2 in the ground. It was right around here that the first humans appeared. Notice that you can reach back and almost touch the first sign. This represents the total time humans have been on the earth.

3.

Now stretch your legs a bit and take 21 more steps. This will put you in the middle of the Oligocene epoch, smack dab in the middle of the Age of Mammals. Humans are far in the future, but you might run into a giant *Brontotherium* or two, so don't stray far, and stay alert.

14

4.

The Cretaceous period lies another 42 steps down the lane (65 steps from the beginning). It was here, some 65 million years ago, that the last dinosaurs, including some of the most famous, such as *Triceratops* and *Tyrannosaurus*, disappeared.

Keep in mind that it was only after the dinosaurs disappeared that large mammals began to appear. Though mammals had been around for a long time, up to this point they were relatively small. The largest ones were only about the size of a modern badger. In one sense, dinosaur extinction was a lucky break for us. After all, these early mammals were part of the line of evolution that led to you.

5.

From the Cretaceous, take 75 more steps (140 total) to reach the Jurassic period. Here you'll find some *huge* dinosaurs, such as *Apatosaurus* and *Ultrasaurus*. *Allosaurus* was the largest meat eater of this time period, while tiny *Archaeopteryx*, the first bird, was testing its wings.

15

6.

March off another 75 steps (215 total), and you'll find yourself in the middle of the Triassic period. It was right around here that the first dinosaurs appeared. They were small, lightly built animals such as *Coelophysis* that scampered around on two legs. Not too impressive compared to the giants that would come later.

Stop here for a moment and look back to sign number 3, which marks the end of the Cretaceous period. The space you are looking at is the Age of the Dinosaurs, and it lasted at least 150 million years.

Now think about the distance that human history occupies on your time line—you could practically reach from one end of it to the other without taking a step. Of course, our story isn't over yet, but when you look at it in this light, which animals would you consider more successful, dinosaurs or humans?

7.

Our next step is just 30 short steps (245 total) away. This point marks the beginning of the Triassic period. Together, the Triassic, Jurassic, and Cretaceous periods make up the Mesozoic era, one of the four great divisions in the earth's history. The Mesozoic era is often called the Age of Reptiles.

The dinosaurs were still far in the future, but there were some great animals running around 245 million years ago. The giant, crocodilelike phytosaurs, for example, lived in freshwater streams and lakes, while massive placodonts swam in shallow marine waters.

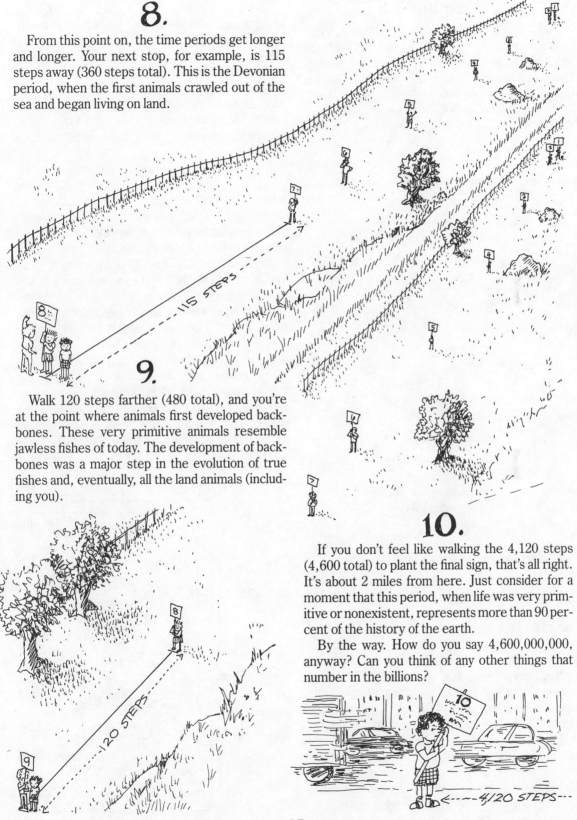

8.

From this point on, the time periods get longer and longer. Your next stop, for example, is 115 steps away (360 steps total). This is the Devonian period, when the first animals crawled out of the sea and began living on land.

9.

Walk 120 steps farther (480 total), and you're at the point where animals first developed backbones. These very primitive animals resemble jawless fishes of today. The development of backbones was a major step in the evolution of true fishes and, eventually, all the land animals (including you).

10.

If you don't feel like walking the 4,120 steps (4,600 total) to plant the final sign, that's all right. It's about 2 miles from here. Just consider for a moment that this period, when life was very primitive or nonexistent, represents more than 90 percent of the history of the earth.

By the way. How do you say 4,600,000,000, anyway? Can you think of any other things that number in the billions?

Beast Boxes

Can you tell where science ends and science fiction begins? Scattered throughout this book you'll find Beast Boxes that profile some mighty strange dinosaurs. Most of them are real, but one is imaginary. As you look through the book, keep an eye out for the "bogus beast." Everything about it is somehow wrong.

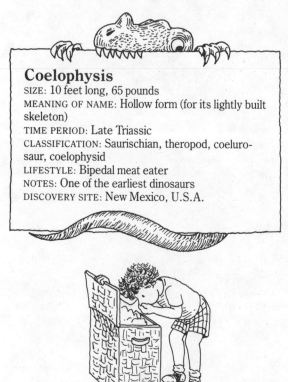

Coelophysis
SIZE: 10 feet long, 65 pounds
MEANING OF NAME: Hollow form (for its lightly built skeleton)
TIME PERIOD: Late Triassic
CLASSIFICATION: Saurischian, theropod, coelurosaur, coelophysid
LIFESTYLE: Bipedal meat eater
NOTES: One of the earliest dinosaurs
DISCOVERY SITE: New Mexico, U.S.A.

How Geologists Tell Time

Consider your laundry hamper for a moment. Think about the clothes you threw into the hamper three days ago and those that you put in there last night. Assuming that no one has done the laundry in the meantime, what can you say about the two days' worth of laundry?

No, I don't mean that some are mustier than others. What can you say about where they lie in relationship to each other? Go ahead, dive in and see where things are.

Most likely, the clothes you threw in three days ago are lower in the hamper than those you threw in last night. This, of course, assumes that your dad didn't stir up the whole thing when he was looking for his favorite work shirt this morning.

And this brings us to our point. Normally, the rocks in the earth are layered just like the laundry in your hamper. Those that were formed first, just like the clothes that were thrown in first, usually lie below those that formed more recently.

I say usually because just as your dad can disturb clothes as he rummages around for his shirt, earthquakes, volcanoes, and mountain ranges can also turn rock layers upside down or tilt them on their sides.

Just as you wear different kinds of clothes depending on the weather, layers of rock, called *strata*, also vary depending on the weather conditions under which they form. These strata form a time line that scientists use to determine which part of the earth's history they're looking at. Scientists who study the history of the earth by looking at strata and what they contain are called stratigraphers.

Exploring Your Laundry Hamper. Let's take an imaginary tour of your laundry hamper—down through the layers of clothes to those you wore three days ago. By looking at them closely, you could probably tell a lot about what happened the day you wore them. There's the chocolate sauce you spilled on your school clothes at lunch, and there's the dirt stain on the elbow of your baseball jersey where you slid into second base.

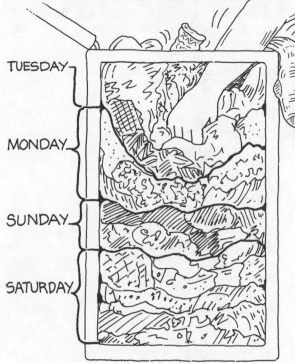

TUESDAY

MONDAY

SUNDAY

SATURDAY

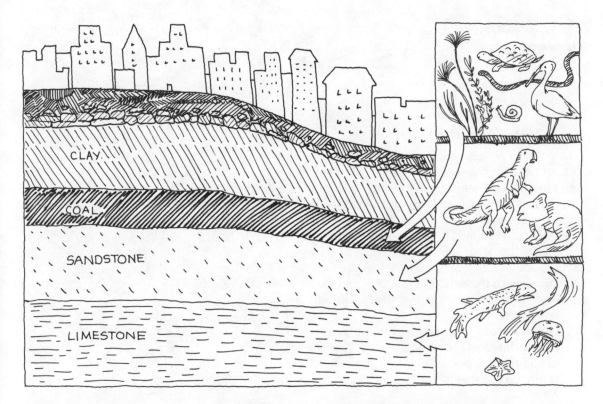

In the same way, stratigraphers try to reconstruct what happened millions of years ago when the rock strata were laid down. The position, texture, and composition of each stratum say a lot about what was happening.

The stratum's position, as we mentioned, determines its age *relative* to the strata above and below it. It doesn't tell us how old a rock is, but just that it's older than the strata above it and younger than the strata below it. This is called *relative dating*.

The stratum's texture and composition tell how it was formed. Sedimentary rocks, for example, are formed from sand, silt, and rocks that have been washed into low-lying areas. Over time, these sediments get deeper and deeper. As more layers collect, they become very heavy. Gradually, they squash the lower layers so tightly together that all the water is forced out. New chemical processes occur, and the particles combine to form rocks.

If the original sediment particles were sand, the rock that forms is sandstone. If they were silt, it becomes siltstone. If they were clay it becomes claystone or chert. And if the strata were made of particles larger than sand, the rock formed is called *conglomerate*.

Animal and plant remains can also be covered and squashed under the same pressures. The shells of some sea animals, for example, form limestone or marble. What was once an ancient swamp might be compressed and eventually become a coal bed.

So what does all that have to do with dinosaurs? Just this. Rock strata are the street signs for time-traveling scientists such as geologists and paleontologists. When they go looking for a certain kind of prehistoric animal, they know to look for strata that formed at the time the animal was alive. There are some layers of strata, called *formations*, that are well known among paleontologists for the fossils they contain.

For example, the Morrison formation (named for the town in Colorado near where it was first recognized) is famous for late Jurassic dinosaurs such as *Stegosaurus* and *Camarasaurus*. Dinosaur National Monument, which straddles the Colorado/Utah border, contains rocks from the Morrison formation.

The Judith River (or Oldman) formation in Montana is another famous example. It contains late Cretaceous dinosaurs such as *Triceratops* and *Tyrannosaurus*, as well as duck-billed dinosaurs such as *Lambeosaurus* and *Parasaurolophus*.

19

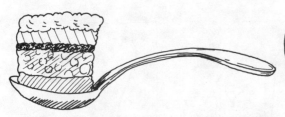

Geology You Can Eat

One way to get a good look at what happens to rock strata is to make your own. You could do it with sand, silt, and seashells, but then you'd have to wait around for thousands of years before you could see the results.

A much quicker way is to use flavored gelatin—you know, the kind your mom keeps in the kitchen. It's easy to make; it's a lot less messy; and when you're through looking it over and experimenting with it, you can eat what's left for dessert. **You will need:**

> **three flavors of gelatin—maybe raspberry, lime, and lemon**
> **graham crackers**
> **whipped cream**
> **banana**
> **clear Pyrex or glass pan, 8 inches by 12 inches and at least 2 inches deep**
> **measuring cup**

First, mix up a batch of limestone, more commonly known as lime gelatin. We'll say that this stratum formed when the area was under the ocean. To create the limestone, put the gelatin in a measuring cup, add boiling water, and stir. Add a little less water than called for in the directions on the box. Let your limestone cool in the mixing cup for about 15 minutes, then pour it into the pan. Place the pan so it is level in the refrigerator and leave it until the gelatin is completely set.

Next, make a stratum of sandstone, the kind that forms from sand deposited by a river. Fossils are often found in this kind of stratum, so we'll need some fossils too. In this case, the sandstone will be raspberry gelatin and the fossils will be pieces of banana.

Cut the banana into small chunks. Mix the gelatin in the measuring cup as you did before and let it cool for about 12 minutes. Mix in the banana. Pour this mixture into the pan on top of the "limestone." Make sure the limestone is completely firm, so the two layers don't mix together. Place the pan back in the refrigerator until it is cold and firm.

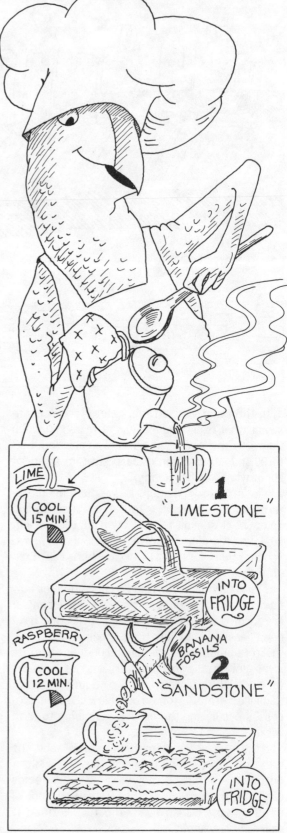

LIME COOL 15 MIN.

1 "LIMESTONE"

INTO FRIDGE

RASPBERRY COOL 12 MIN.

BANANA FOSSILS

2 "SANDSTONE"

INTO FRIDGE

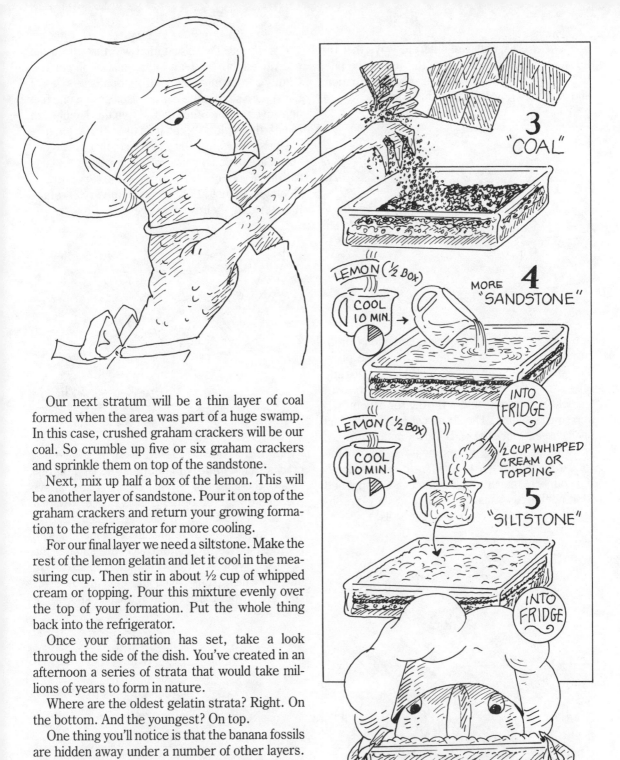

3 "COAL"

LEMON (½ BOX)
COOL 10 MIN.

MORE "SANDSTONE"

4

INTO FRIDGE

LEMON (½ BOX)
COOL 10 MIN.

½ CUP WHIPPED CREAM OR TOPPING

5 "SILTSTONE"

INTO FRIDGE

Our next stratum will be a thin layer of coal formed when the area was part of a huge swamp. In this case, crushed graham crackers will be our coal. So crumble up five or six graham crackers and sprinkle them on top of the sandstone.

Next, mix up half a box of the lemon. This will be another layer of sandstone. Pour it on top of the graham crackers and return your growing formation to the refrigerator for more cooling.

For our final layer we need a siltstone. Make the rest of the lemon gelatin and let it cool in the measuring cup. Then stir in about ½ cup of whipped cream or topping. Pour this mixture evenly over the top of your formation. Put the whole thing back into the refrigerator.

Once your formation has set, take a look through the side of the dish. You've created in an afternoon a series of strata that would take millions of years to form in nature.

Where are the oldest gelatin strata? Right. On the bottom. And the youngest? On top.

One thing you'll notice is that the banana fossils are hidden away under a number of other layers. How will they ever be found? Fortunately, things don't stay put in nature. Rock strata may not be as soft as gelatin, but they do stretch and bend and even break, just like gelatin layers, when they are subjected to the heat and pressure generated by the earth.

21

There are a number of different ways that the fossils can work their way to the top of the pile. Cut a 4-inch-by-4-inch square of the formation, and you'll see how this might happen.

Uplifting. First, there are tremendous pressures building up inside the earth. These pressures form mountain ranges, and at the same time they twist flat strata into all sorts of bizarre shapes. Slide a knife under the center of your gelatin square and lift. The strata will bend so far and finally break. Once the pieces are standing on end, you'll see something interesting—one edge of the sandstone with the fossils is now on the surface. If a couple of miniature paleontologists happened to wander across this area right now, they'd probably discover some great banana fossils!

Let's try up there.

Looks good.

Looks sticky.

Overthrust. There's another way that strata can get mixed up. Cut another square of gelatin. Gently and evenly push in from opposite sides of the square so that the center rises up and one half flops over on the other half. When this happens in the earth, geologists call it an *overthrust.*

One interesting thing. Notice that the older strata are no longer under younger ones. In fact, half of the youngest stratum is on the very bottom. Geologists must study rock strata very carefully to determine their relative ages.

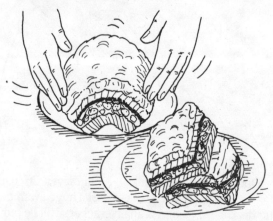

Faulting. The surface of the earth is full of big cracks called *faults.* Sometimes the land on one side of the fault will be uplifted, or raised, above the land on the other side. This is one way that fossils can work their way to the surface.

You can demonstrate the effects of faulting with another square of gelatin. Slice the square into two parts with a spatula. Then use the spatula to lift up one half. If it is raised high enough, the layer containing your fossil bananas will be exposed.

Erosion. Fortunately for paleontologists, sedimentary rocks are constantly being worn away from above by wind and rain, so fossils are constantly being uncovered. We can show this with a cupful of warm water and another square of stratified gelatin.

Place the gelatin on the paper towel on a plate. Tilt the plate over a sink or bowl, which will catch the water, and slowly pour a stream of warm water on one edge. Gradually, the top layers will melt away, exposing the fossil (banana) layer.

The wind also erodes sediments. To show this, take a blow dryer, turn it to warm, and aim it at a square of gelatin. In a few minutes the top layers will begin to dissolve. Soon banana fossils will be uncovered. (Of course, in nature the rocks don't melt. They're just slowly broken down and carried away.)

Notice how small pieces of banana flow out with the melting gelatin. This happens with real fossils too. When paleontologists find a few small bone fragments lying on the ground (which they call *float*), they often find the rest of the fossil by looking in the rocks directly above it.

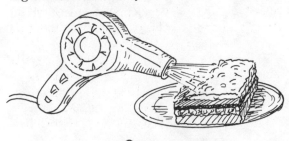

Camarasaurus

SIZE: 60 feet long, 20 tons
MEANING OF NAME: Chambered lizard (for the hollow chambers in its backbone)
TIME PERIOD: Late Jurassic
CLASSIFICATION: Saurischian, sauropodamorph, sauropod, camarasaurid
LIFESTYLE: Browsed on leaves in high trees
NOTES: Big nostrils on top of head make some people think it had a trunk
DISCOVERY SITE: Colorado, U.S.A.

Marker Beds. Coal beds like the one formed by your graham crackers are very important to paleontologists because they can be seen very easily. A gelatin geologist looking at your formation, for example, could always be sure that wherever she spotted graham crackers she would also be likely to find bananas in the next layer. Real fossil hunters often use the dark black coal beds as "markers" because they are easy to spot among all the light gray and brown layers. By knowing where the fossil-rich strata are in relation to the coal, they can zero in on the areas where they are most likely to find fossils.

Looking for Stone Rainbows

Next time you take a drive into the countryside with your family, look for rock strata along the sides of the road. Engineers love to build flat roads. Instead of putting a road over a hill, they'd rather cut straight through it. This is great for paleontologists because road cuts often expose very interesting rocks, and sometimes even fossils. Look closely at the sides of road cuts the next time you're on a trip. The strata in a hillside sometimes form beautiful arcs, just like rainbows made of stone!

23

Mixing Up the Mesozoic

Let's test your sense of time. Can you see anything wrong with this picture? You're right if you said the girl doesn't belong in the same picture with the dinosaurs. But that's not all. None of the animals should be shown with any of the others. Each one lived millions of years away from the others.

The small dinosaur, *Coelophysis* lived in the Triassic period 220 million years ago. *Stegosaurus* lived in the Jurassic period 150 million years ago. *Triceratops* lived in the Cretaceous period 65 million years ago. And the girl? She's alive right now.

If you think about it, putting the three dinosaurs together in the same illustration makes even less sense than putting the girl with *Tyrannosaurus*. After all, only 65 million years separate the girl from the *Tyrannosaurus rex*, while more than 150 million years separate the earliest dinosaurs from the latest dinosaurs.

24

Here's a chart to help you keep your dinosaurs in the right time period. As you learn about new ones, add them to the chart to see which other dinosaurs lived in the same time periods.

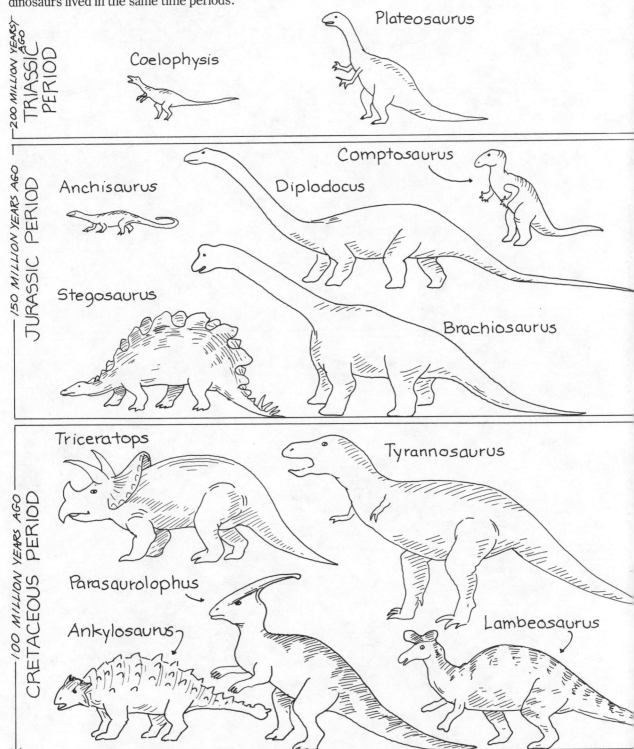

200 MILLION YEARS AGO
TRIASSIC PERIOD

Coelophysis

Plateosaurus

150 MILLION YEARS AGO
JURASSIC PERIOD

Anchisaurus

Diplodocus

Comptosaurus

Stegosaurus

Brachiosaurus

100 MILLION YEARS AGO
CRETACEOUS PERIOD

Triceratops

Tyrannosaurus

Parasaurolophus

Ankylosaurus

Lambeosaurus

25

Now look at these two illustrations and pick out
the dinosaurs that don't belong.

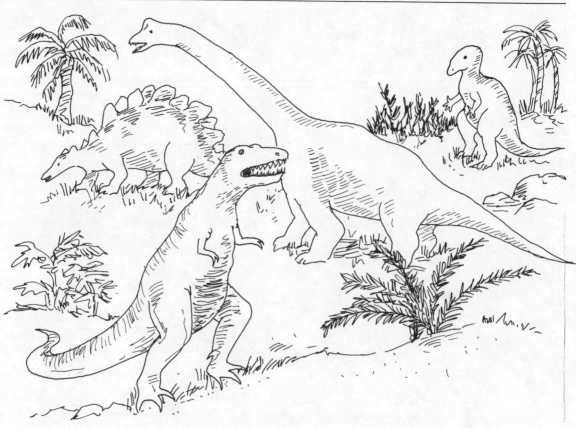

Rock Solid

Now that you've tinkered with your sense of time, you should probably also do a little fine tuning in another area that you also take for granted—the continents. They may seem unchangeable when you look at them on a map, but they're actually moving, ever so slowly, all the time. And when you start thinking geologically about time, these slight movements add up to huge changes.

Here's an exercise for you to consider. If you have a pool or swimming hole and want to try it out, go ahead. Otherwise, just think about what will happen.

Catch My Drift? You and six friends are floating on air mattresses. You scatter yourselves out along every side of the pool. Then each person picks a point on the opposite side of the pool and starts paddling toward it. What happens?

Most likely, you'll end up with a giant collision, an "air mattress jam," somewhere near the center of the pool. Well, the earth's crust is made up of giant plates called *tectonic plates*. These plates float on a sea of molten rock, and they're always moving. As they move, they carry the seven continents with them. It happens very, very slowly, about two inches a year, but it never stops. Over millions of years, the continents are rearranged as if they were moving around on giant conveyor belts. This is called *continental drift*.

Remember the air mattress jam? Well, 200 million years ago, in the early Jurassic period, when the dinosaurs first appeared, there was a giant continent jam. All of the continents had collided, creating a giant landmass called Pangaea.

When continents are connected, animals move freely from one to another. It's just like in the swimming pool. When all the air mattresses are pushed together, it's easy for you to hop onto somebody else's mattress. During their time on the earth, the dinosaurs did a lot of continent hopping.

Eventually, Pangaea broke up. About 180 million years ago it divided into two large landmasses: South America, Africa (with India still connected), Antarctica, and Australia pulled away from Europe and North America. A shallow sea isolated Asia. By 135 million years ago, in the early Cretaceous, South America and Africa had split apart. India had left Africa and was headed toward Asia. By 65 million years ago, the end of the Cretaceous period, when the dinosaurs disappeared, the Atlantic Ocean had grown quite large, separating South America from Africa.

Today, the process continues. The Atlantic Ocean gets wider ever so slowly. Australia inches northward. And southern California moves toward Alaska. In ten million years, Los Angeles will be even with San Francisco on its long journey north.

Dinosaurs Adrift. Continental drift helps explain why dinosaur fossils are distributed around the world—from the Arctic to the Antarctic. It also explains why you often find similar dinosaurs in surprising places. You find dinosaurs in Antarctica because it was once connected to the other continents, and it wasn't always located at such an extreme latitude.

You also find similar kinds of dinosaurs in Montana and China—these two areas were linked for long periods of time. You find very different dinosaurs in the eastern United States, which was isolated by a great inland sea.

These maps will show you where the continents were during each period of the Mesozoic era.

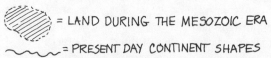

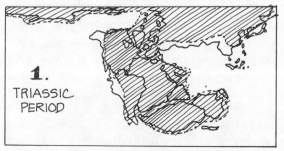

1.
TRIASSIC
PERIOD

2.
JURASSIC
PERIOD

3.
EARLY
CRETACEOUS
PERIOD

4.
LATE
CRETACEOUS
PERIOD

Aloha! No, there aren't any dinosaurs in Hawaii, but if you want to get an idea of which way one tectonic plate is moving, grab a map and look for these islands. From their base, 18,000 feet under the water, to the highest point, just over 10,000 feet, they are actually the tallest mountains in the world.

The islands were created as the mid-Pacific plate was dragged slowly over a hot spot in the earth's crust. The oldest of the major islands is Kauai (5 to 6 million years), in the far northwest. Then came Oahu (2 to 3 million), then Maui (1 million), and then Hawaii (less than a million years old, with a number of active volcanoes).

As the plate moved over the hot spot, each island was literally "punched out" of the sea floor, providing a directional marker for the northwesterly movement of the plates. This process is continuing today: scientists have found that a new island is beginning to form 30 miles to the southeast of Hawaii.

CHAPTER

2

SORT A SAURUS

There have been a lot of strange creatures during the history of the earth, and not all of them were dinosaurs. Yet most people think anything that's old and scaly is a dinosaur. Not true. The name dinosaur applies only to a very specific group of animals that lived during a certain time period.

Here's a futuristic game show your great grandkids may see on TV someday. Play along, and you'll learn some things that will help you identify a dinosaur the next time you run into one.

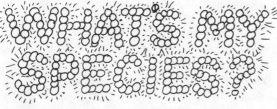

Welcome to "What's My Species?" the game show for the ages. Today, you'll hunt for one of the most famous animals of all times, a dinosaur. Using the wonders of time travel, we've assembled six of the most scaly, downright weird animals that ever lived on the planet Earth.

We'll provide the clues. Your challenge is to use those clues to identify which contestants are dinosaurs. There may be only one dinosaur . . . or they may all be dinosaurs, so choose carefully. If you guess right, you'll win a free, all-expenses-paid trip back to the late Cretaceous period. There you'll dine with *Deinonychus*, migrate with *Maiasaura*, and enjoy an evening under the stars watching the meteor showers.

Now, let's meet our contestants...

Ready? Here are the clues:

Clue No. 1. Dinosaurs really existed. They all lived during the Mesozoic era, which ended 65 million years ago. They didn't breathe fire, and they didn't rise out of the ocean to terrorize actors in science fiction films.

Clue No. 2. Dinosaurs lived primarily on land. Just like humans or elephants, some may have gone into the water for short periods, but they were most at home on land. They moved around on well-developed legs rather than using flippers to swim or wings to fly.

Clue No. 3. This is a bit technical, but it's also very important. Dinosaurs were diapsids. That means they had two telltale openings in their skulls. The openings were located directly behind the eye holes, stacked one on top of the other. They made the animals' skulls lighter and also pro-

vided areas around the edges of the holes where the jaw muscles attached. This gave the dinosaurs powerful jaw muscles for chewing their food. Obviously we'll need X-rays of the suspects' skulls. Here are the results:

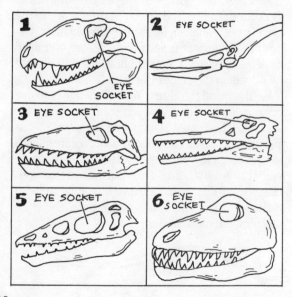

Clue No. 4. Look at the animals' legs again. Dinosaurs walked with their legs directly under their bodies. Up until the time of the dinosaurs, most animals' legs sprawled out to the side like those of a lizard. Because they had open hip sockets, dinosaurs were able to carry their legs directly under their bodies, so they could run much faster.

31

Clue No. 1 shows that Contestant 6 is a fake. This animal existed only in science fiction films. We call this fire-breathing nightmare Godzilla!

Clue No. 2 eliminates Contestants 2 and 3. The giant wings on 2 tell you that it's a pterosaur, a flying reptile. And the paddles on Contestant 3 show that it lived in the water. It's a plesiosaur, a marine reptile. Neither is a dinosaur.

Clue No. 4 states that dinosaurs were diapsids, so the X-rays reveal one more imposter. Contestant 1 has only one opening in its skull. It's not a dinosaur at all, but *Dimetrodon*, a mammallike reptile that lived millions of years before the dinosaurs. Much later, the relatives of *Dimetron* evolved into the first true mammals.

We're now down to two contestants. Which animal carries its legs directly under its body? Surely not Contestant 4. That is a phytosaur, one of the early thecodonts that were the ancestors of the dinosaurs.

You win if you picked Contestant 5. Little *Compsognathus* is the only dinosaur in the group. It may have been small, but don't be fooled by its size. *Compsognathus* was a fast and deadly predator that caught lizards and other small prey with its sharp claws and teeth.

Defining Dinosaurs

It was pretty sneaky to try to fool you by using a turkey-size dinosaur for the game show. But it's important to remember that dinosaurs didn't always look the way we expect them to. In fact, they often looked very different from one another.

What did they have in common? Here's a definition based on "What's My Species?":

•Dinosaurs.• They were a group of animals that lived during the Mesozoic era. They lived primarily on land, walked with their legs under their bodies, and had skulls with similar openings.

Here's a game that will show you another reason why dinosaurs are grouped together.

Related Strangers. We'll call it the Game of Related Strangers. Here are two four-letter words. By changing one letter at a time, try to bridge the gap between the two words. The trick is that each of the steps between the two words must also be a word. Here's an example: the challenge is to change DINO (we'll call it a word) to BIRD. And here's the solution:

DINO
DING
RING
RIND
BIND
BIRD

We've changed a dinosaur (or at least a dino) into a bird in five moves! The challenge is to make the change in the fewest possible moves. In this case, that would be four moves. Grab a piece of paper and try to link these words together: NINE–SAVE, DRIP–SEAM, RARE–FILM.

Make up other word pairs and with your friends see if you can link the two words. Try it with five-letter words. It gets a lot harder.

"Good game," you say, "but what does it have to do with dinosaurs?" Everything. Dinosaurs were on the earth for about 160 million years. During that time they changed very, very gradually into animals that were completely different from each other. Some became tremendously large, while others remained very small. Some had sharp teeth for tearing flesh, while others developed short beaks for clipping off plants. Some were very fast. Others were slow, lumbering creatures. But they still had their ancestry in common: all dinosaurs evolved from the same group of animals.

Think about the Game of Related Strangers for a moment. Every letter in the beginning and ending words is different. At first glance two words couldn't seem much more different. But you know that they are related, that one evolved out of the other and that each step between them was a word in itself.

Just as you can make a completely different word by changing one letter at a time, the dinosaurs evolved into very different animals one step at a time. These changes were small at first, but as time went on the differences between the dinosaurs became greater. And all along the way each linking step was filled by an animal.

Over 160 million years the differences became very great. About 300 species of dinosaurs have been identified up to now, and more are being discovered all the time. How do scientists keep all these animals straight? They organize them into smaller groups, of course. That's what we'll look at next.

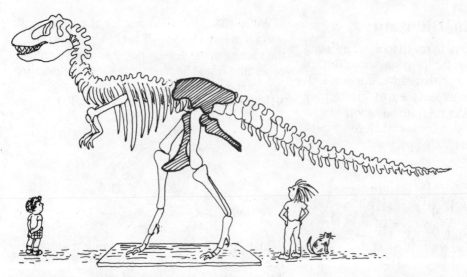

Shooting from the Hip. The animals that we call dinosaurs are actually classified into two different groups based on their hip (or pelvic) structure. Why their hips? Remember that one reason dinosaurs were so successful was that, with their legs directly under their bodies, they could run very fast. Speed was possible because their hipbones and legbones were different from those of earlier animals.

There are three main bones in a dinosaur's hip. The ilium, the ischium, and the pubis. All dinosaurs have these bones, but they can be shaped very differently. In some dinosaurs the pubis points forward, while the ischium points backward. Most lizards have hipbones like this, so these dinosaurs are called *saurischians*, which means "lizard hips."

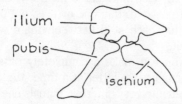

In other dinosaurs, both the pubis and the ischium point backward. This arrangement is similar to modern birds, so this group is called the *ornithischians*, or "bird hips." Their hips looked something like this:

Look closely at the skeleton of *Tyrannosaurus*. Is it an ornithischian or a saurischian? Right, *Tyrannosaurus* was a saurischian. You can tell because the pubis points forward.

The pelvic bones of individual dinosaurs vary a bit, but they all fit into these two general groups. Here is an assortment of hipbones from different dinosaurs. Try sorting them into saurischians and ornithischians.

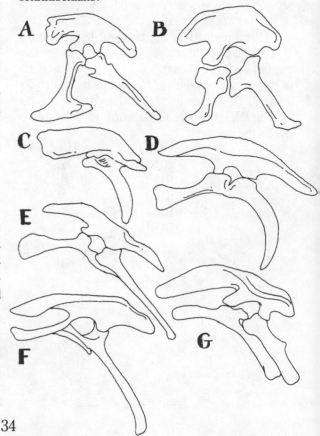

34

You were right if you said that A and B are saurischians, while C, D, E, F, and G are ornithischians. In fact, if you flesh out the dinosaurs that belong to these bones, you'll see the seven suborders of dinosaurs.

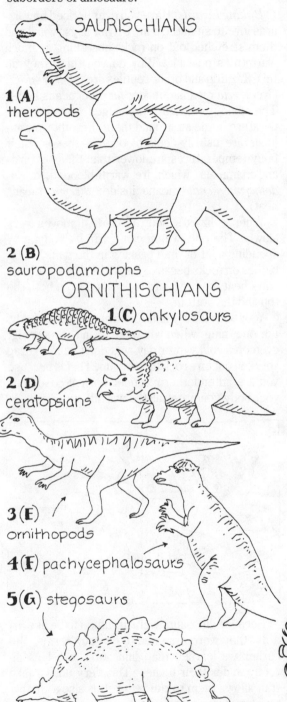

SAURISCHIANS

1 (A) theropods

2 (B) sauropodamorphs

ORNITHISCHIANS

1 (C) ankylosaurs

2 (D) ceratopsians

3 (E) ornithopods

4 (F) pachycephalosaurs

5 (G) stegosaurs

The saurischians include:

1. theropods—the only meat-eating dinosaurs. This group includes small dinosaurs such as *Compsognathus* as well as large ones like *Tyrannosaurus*

2. sauropodamorphs—the giant plant eaters such as *Apatosaurus* and *Brachiosaurus*.

The ornithischians were all plant eaters. They include:

1. ankylosaurs—armor-plated dinosaurs

2. ceratopsians—dinosaurs with large horns and frills

3. ornithopods—includes many different plant eaters, including the duck-billed dinosaurs (hadrosaurs)

4. pachycephalosaurs—dinosaurs with thick, bony skulls

5. stegosaurs—dinosaurs with large plates or spikes on their backs.

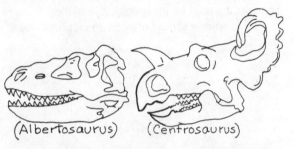

(Albertosaurus)   (Centrosaurus)

Jaws. There's one other way to tell the difference between ornithischian and saurischian dinosaurs. That's to look at their jawbones. Ornithischians have beaklike bones in front of their teeth. This bone is called a *predentary*, and it clipped off the plants that all ornithischian dinosaurs ate.

What Were Dinosaurs Like? Scientists are always comparing dinosaurs to modern animals. When Richard Owen invented the word *dinosaur* in 1841, he imagined them to be like overgrown lizards that lumbered around on four legs. When he hit upon the word *dinosaur*, which, you remember, means "terrible lizard" in Greek, he thought it would be an appropriate name for animals that were a cross between an elephant and a lizard.

After more fossils had been found, some scientists began to doubt Owen's vision of elephantine lizards. One such scientist was Joseph Leidy, the father of American paleontology. In 1858 Leidy looked at the massive rear legs and tiny forelegs of the first dinosaur skeleton found in the United States and thought the animal must have been more like a modern kangaroo.

Analogies to modern animals ("Dinosaurs are like . . .") help scientists explain their ideas about dinosaurs, but analogies can also be misleading. Because Owen initially thought dinosaurs were like lizards, most people have assumed they had all the reptilian characteristics. But now scientists are starting to question this idea. Here's one reason why.

Baking Lizards. Have you ever noticed how lizards love to sit in the sun? On hot days, you'll find them stretched out on rocks absorbing as much warmth as possible. Why do you think they do this? Lizards and other reptiles are *ectothermic* (in Greek *ecto* means outside; *thermic* means heat). Their body temperature changes with the temperature of the air around them. Ectothermic animals are usually "cold-blooded"—that is, their body temperatures are lower than those of birds and mammals, which are warm-blooded, or *endothermic* (*endo* means inside; *thermic* means heat).

When a lizard's body is cold, it moves very slowly. The only way it can warm its body is by spending a lot of time basking in the sun. It sunbathes on rocks because the rocks also absorb the sun's heat, so the lizard is warmed from both the top and the bottom.

Your body is very different from a reptile's body. For one thing, when you wake up in the morning, even on a cold winter day, you don't have to drag yourself out on a rock to warm up. That is because you are an endotherm: under normal conditions your body generates all the warmth it needs.

Because dinosaurs were assumed to be like lizards, they were assumed to be ectotherms. But earlier we learned that dinosaurs have legs directly under their bodies. This very unlizardlike trait allows them to run faster. It is also a characteristic usually found only in endotherms. It takes a lot of energy to hold your body high off the ground, and only endotherms can produce it.

This characteristic set a number of scientists to thinking about whether dinosaurs really were ectotherms, and if so, how they fit into the reptile category. The illustrations show some of the traits of a common reptile (a lizard), a bird (an ostrich), and a dinosaur (*Struthiomimus*).

Look at the illustrations carefully. The chart will help show you what to look for. Then use a pencil and a sheet of paper to note the ways in which dinosaurs are like the other animals. In one column list the ways in which they are like reptiles. In another column note their similarities to birds. Then decide for yourself: Were dinosaurs more like reptiles or more like birds?

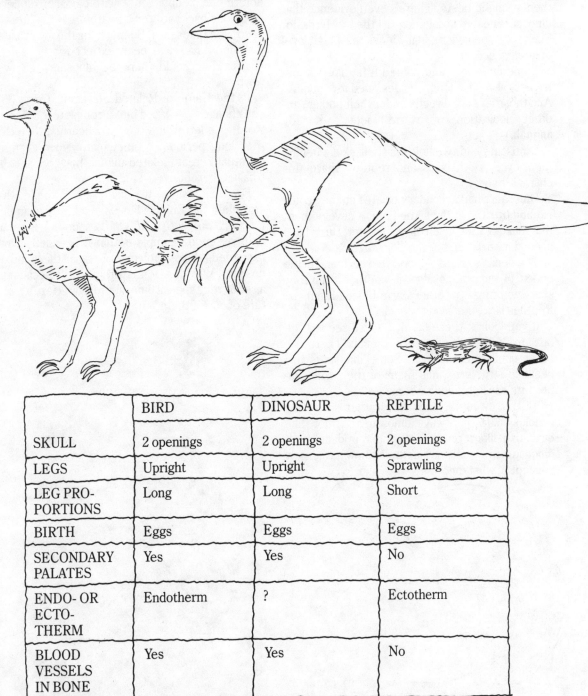

	BIRD	DINOSAUR	REPTILE
SKULL	2 openings	2 openings	2 openings
LEGS	Upright	Upright	Sprawling
LEG PRO-PORTIONS	Long	Long	Short
BIRTH	Eggs	Eggs	Eggs
SECONDARY PALATES	Yes	Yes	No
ENDO- OR ECTO-THERM	Endotherm	?	Ectotherm
BLOOD VESSELS IN BONE	Yes	Yes	No

As you can see, dinosaurs share traits with both kinds of animals, reptiles and birds. In this case, *Struthiomimus* shares a number of traits with birds that are usually found only in warm-blooded animals.

Most dinosaurs laid eggs, as do reptiles and birds, but only some dinosaurs and birds cared for their young in nests. There's even evidence that dinosaurs nested in colonies just the way birds do. Such social behavior usually indicates a high level of intelligence.

Some dinosaurs and some birds (like the ostriches) also have long legs designed for running. And these legs are directly under their bodies, another indication of warm-blooded, speedy animals.

Dinosaurs had two holes in their skulls behind their eyes. Both birds and reptiles share this characteristic.

Dinosaurs had secondary palates so they could eat and breathe at the same time, a development that makes eating much more efficient. Birds have secondary palates, but reptiles don't.

The dense system of blood vessels found in the bones of many dinosaurs is another trait they share with birds and other warm-blooded animals. Reptiles lack such blood vessels.

If you look at these factors, you'll see that dinosaurs and birds are very similar. There are other similarities as well. Some dinosaurs had beaklike structures, and many of the smaller dinosaurs had light, hollow bones.

All this evidence leads to a rather surprising conclusion. In many ways, dinosaurs are more like birds than like reptiles. This puts our ideas about dinosaurs in a whole new light. We now have a new concept of what dinosaurs were like.

For the Birds

Paleontologists go even further than saying dinosaurs were like birds. They say that living birds *are* dinosaurs. That's right. The national symbol of the United States is a dinosaur. Each year in November people all over the United States celebrate our independence with dinosaur dinners. And your backyard (or a nearby park) is literally filled with dinosaurs! So much for the idea that all the dinosaurs have been extinct for 65 million years. How could there be dinosaurs all over town?

In the Game of Related Strangers (page 33), you changed one word into a completely different word, one letter at a time. You learned then that over long periods of time, many small changes eventually create related animals that appear to be totally different.

For that game we used an example that stretched the English language a bit by changing the word *dino* into *bird*. One reason this is a particularly good example is that it is exactly what happened—birds evolved from small theropod dinosaurs. Why do scientists think this? Because of a set of very special dinosaur fossils. Here's a picture of one of them.

Do you notice anything special about this fossil that makes it different from other dinosaur fossils? In 1861 this nearly complete skeleton was found by workers in a German quarry. The skeleton looks like a small bipedal dinosaur because it has both a long tail and clawed fingers. But there's one big difference. Impressed on the stone around the fossil are the imprints of feathers.

The animal is called *Archaeopteryx*, which means "old feather." It is the evolutionary link between dinosaurs and birds. After the discovery of *Archaeopteryx*, scientists began to notice a number of other similarities between small dinosaurs and birds—the hollow bones, the light skeletal structures, the relatively long hind limbs, and the long narrow tails.

This connection, as well as an increased awareness of the differences between modern reptiles and dinosaurs, has led some scientists to conclude that the groups we use to categorize animals should be changed. Rather than putting dinosaurs into the reptile category and birds into their own category, the two should be combined into a single category—the dinosauria.

The Feathered Reptiles. We usually think of feathers and scales as being very different. That's not really the case. In fact, birds are covered mostly in feathers, but what kind of covering do they have on their legs? Right. They have scales. In many ways, birds are feathered reptiles. There's also one animal living in Antarctica today that has both feathers and scales on its wings. What is this creature? The penguin. Feathers are just fancy scales designed for a specific purpose. What is that purpose? That's what we'll look at next.

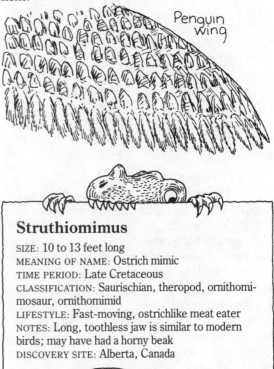

Penguin wing

Struthiomimus

SIZE: 10 to 13 feet long
MEANING OF NAME: Ostrich mimic
TIME PERIOD: Late Cretaceous
CLASSIFICATION: Saurischian, theropod, ornithomimosaur, ornithomimid
LIFESTYLE: Fast-moving, ostrichlike meat eater
NOTES: Long, toothless jaw is similar to modern birds; may have had a horny beak
DISCOVERY SITE: Alberta, Canada

Why Did Feathers Evolve? What good are feathers? Especially for a dinosaur that didn't have a skeleton or muscles that would let it fly? For one thing, feathers hold in heat. They evolved to let small dinosaurs cope with heat loss. But the logic of this argument demands a dramatic rethinking of our view of dinosaurs. If dinosaurs were cold-blooded like reptiles, their bodies wouldn't need feathers. There wouldn't be any heat to hold in. In fact, feathers would block the sun, preventing a cold-blooded dinosaur from warming itself. Feathers make sense only if the dinosaur was already endothermic (warm-blooded).

1. Once you've located a print, form the paper into a ring just large enough to surround the print. Use the paper clip to hold the two ends of the paper together.

2. Place the ring around the print.

3. Add water to the plaster of paris and stir. Make it a bit thinner than the directions on the package call for. Pour the plaster into the print.

4. Take a hike and do some dinosaur observing while the plaster dries.

Pigeon-Toed or Dino-Toed? Compare the footprints. The ones on the left were made by a coelurosaur, the ones on the right by a modern bird. Except for the size, there are many similarities. Both animals have three toes with the middle toe the longest. And both animals turn their toes slightly inward to maintain their balance. So, in a sense, your pigeon-toed sister really is dino-toed!

If you live near Hartford, Connecticut, you can make a print of a real dinosaur's footprint (see page 64). But even if you live at the other end of the country, you can cast the footprints of birds, the living dinosaurs.

First, you'll have to do a bit of prospecting. Look for a place with damp, soft ground—a beach or muddy streambank is perfect, but you might also look around mud puddles after a rainstorm.

You will need:
> **plaster of paris**
> **water**
> **a strip of heavy paper about 4 inches by 12 inches**
> **a paper clip**
> **a can and a stick for mixing up the plaster**
> **Vaseline**
> **tape**
> **newspaper**

The dried plaster will form a mold of the print. You can color the raised portion of the print with a felt marker to make it stand out. And if you'd like a positive image, or cast, just do this:

1. Rub Vaseline on the top of the mold. This will keep the two halves from sticking together.

2. Put the ring back around your mold. You might use tape to hold the paper tightly in place. And be sure to put newspapers underneath.

3. Pour in additional plaster. Let it dry thoroughly.

4. Separate the two halves. The cast should be an exact copy of the original footprint.

You can make a collection of dinosaur footprints. Each time you make one try to figure out which bird . . . I mean dinosaur . . . made the print. (One of the most difficult tasks paleontologists have is trying to relate dinosaur footprints to the animals that made them.) You might also keep a record of when and where the print was made.

Noah's Ravens

Pliny Moody was only 12 years old, but he was already working hard to help out on the family farm. The year was 1802. The place was western Massachusetts. One day, when Pliny was tilling a field, his plow turned up something very strange. It was a flat piece of stone with footprints on it. The footprints looked like they had been made by a bird, except they were much too large.

Pliny told people about his discovery. Because people didn't yet know about dinosaurs—remember, the word *dinosaur* wasn't even invented until 1841—they thought the prints must have been made by giant ravens that Noah let loose from the Ark after the great flood in the Bible. News of the find spread like wildfire, and crowds "flocked" to see the footprints made by "Noah's ravens."

The prints also caught the attention of Edward Hitchcock, the president of Amherst College, who began searching for additional prints. He found what he was looking for. In a search that eventually covered almost the entire Connecticut River Valley and that took 30 years, Hitchcock identified tracks representing 49 species of animals. Thirty-two of these animals walked on two legs with feet that had three or four toes. The largest prints were more than 18 inches long. He called them ornithichites, which is from a Greek word meaning "stony bird tracks."

Hitchcock thought that the prints had been made when the animals had walked on a wet, sandy beach. From studying the prints, he could picture flocks of giant, ostrichlike birds walking along that ancient beach with a number of smaller birds and four-legged animals. Today we know that all the prints Hitchcock studied were made by dinosaurs. So we all owe thanks to 12-year-old Pliny Moody, the hard-working farm boy who uncovered the first dinosaur footprints in America. See what a kid's discovery can lead to!

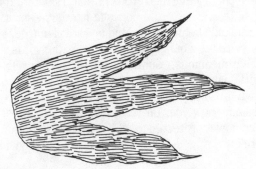

Dinosaur Name Games

Quick, how do you say *Stegosaurus* in Russian? *Stegosaurus*, of course! Dinosaurs lived all over the world, so naturally their fossils are found everywhere now—from Argentina to Alaska, Madagascar to Mongolia, Wyoming to West Germany. They've even found dinosaur fossils in Antarctica. Sometimes it seems like dinosaurs are popping up all over!

Because fossils are scattered over the face of the earth, they're found by scientists who speak every imaginable language. But all paleontologists share a common language. They have to so they can understand what everybody else is talking about! You might call it "dinosaurese."

Names for new dinosaurs, like most scientific names, are usually taken from Latin or ancient Greek. Actually, this is a bit ironic, for the ancient Greeks and Romans (who spoke Latin) never even knew that dinosaurs existed.

When paleontologists discover a new dinosaur, they usually look for its most striking characteristic and give the animal a Latin or Greek name that describes the trait.

41

For example, when a paleontologist discovered a skull in Montana that was 10 inches thick around the brain case, he immediately dubbed it the "thick-headed lizard." But since "thick headed" doesn't sound very scientific (it sounds more like a name you might call your brother), he used the Greek words that mean the same thing. Thus we get *pachy* thick, *cephalo* headed, *saurus* lizard, or *Pachycephalosaurus*.

Dinosaurese can be tricky at first, but once you get used to it, you can have great fun. Here are a few you might like:

DINOSAURS NAMED FOR THEIR HEAD ORNAMENTS

Dilophosaurus	*Di* two, *lopho* ridged, *saurus* lizard
Pachyrhinosaurus	*Pachy* thick, *rhino* nosed
Saurolophus	*Sauro* lizard, *lophus* crested
Tylocephale	*Tylo* knob, *cephale* head
Protoceratops	*Proto* first, *ceratops* horned face
Microceratops	*Micro* small
Triceratops	*Tri* three
Pentaceratops	*Penta* five
Brachyceratops	*Brachy* short

DINOSAURS NAMED FOR THEIR TEETH

Astrodon	*Astro* star, *don* tooth (had unusual-shaped teeth)
Heterodontosaurus	*Hetero* different, *donto* toothed (had two kinds of teeth)
Hypsilophodon	*Hypsi* high, *lopho* ridged
Troödon	*Troo* wounding

DINOSAURS NAMED FOR THEIR FEET

Brachyopodosaurus	*Brachyo* short, *podo* footed
Saltopus	*Salto* leaping, *pus* foot
Velocipes	*Veloci* swift, *pes* foot
Deinonychus	*Deino* terrible, *onychus* claw

DINOSAURS NAMED FOR THEIR BEHAVIOR

Velociraptor	*Veloci* swift, *raptor* thief
Oviraptor	*Ovi* egg
Ornitholestes	*Ornitho* bird, *lestes* robber
Microvenator	*Micro* small, *venator* hunter
Maiasaura	*Maia* good mother
Daspletosaurus	*Daspleto* frightful (had more teeth than *T. rex*)
Tyrannosaurus	*Tyranno* tyrant

DINOSAURS NAMED FOR THEIR BODY FEATURES

Spinosaurus	*Spino* thorn
Altispinax	*Alti* high, *spinax* thorn
Acrocanthosaurus	*Acro* highest, *cantho* spined
Metriacanthosaurus	*Metria* moderately
Styracosaurus	*Styra* spiked
Kentrosaurus	*Kentro* point
Stegosaurus	*Stego* roof
Ankylosaur	*Ankylo* fused
Panoplosaurus	*Panoplo* fully armored

Mix and Match Dinosaurs

All the names above belong to real dinosaurs, but once you get the hang of using Greek and Latin to build words, you can combine the different parts to create new, imaginary dinosaurs. For instance, you might combine: *Nano* dwarf, *pachy* thick, *naso* nosed, *saurus* lizard.

Maybe *Nanopachynasosaurus* had a huge nose, so it could smell dangerous predators before they could get close. And because it was so small, it could hide behind rocks and under fallen trees.

Here are a bunch of Greek and Latin words and their meanings. Combine up to three prefixes (first parts) with a suffix (last part) to create your own imaginary dinosaur. Then write a story explaining how your dinosaur survived, what it ate, and how it protected itself. Outrageous creatures are encouraged. Just be sure you can explain how it lived.

PREFIXES

A	Greek	Without
Alti	Latin	High
Aniso	Greek	Different, unequal
Aqua	Latin	Water
Archi	Greek	Primitive
Atro	Latin	Black
Auri	Latin	Ear
Brachio	Greek	Arm
Caco	Greek	Bad, diseased
Compso	Greek	Elegant
Coelo	Greek	Hollow
Cory	Greek	Helmet
Dactyl	Greek	Finger, toe
Dasy	Greek	Shaggy, hairy
Derma	Greek	Skin
Dextro	Latin	Toward the right
Di	Greek	Two
Dino	Greek	Terrible
Diplo	Greek	Double
Diptera	Greek	With two wings
Dodeca	Greek	Twelve
Ecto	Greek	Outside
Endo	Greek	Inside
Ennea	Greek	Nine
Erythro	Greek	Red
Frigo	Latin	Cold
Hetero	Greek	Different
Hypsi	Greek	High
Labio	Latin	Lips
Lalo	Greek	Babbling
Lepto	Greek	Small, weak
Lophi	Greek	Small crest
Mani	Latin	Hand
Megalo	Greek	Large
Micro	Greek	Small
Mono	Greek	One
Myo	Greek	Mouselike
Myria	Greek	Ten thousand
Myrmeco	Greek	Antlike
Myso	Greek	Unclean
Myxo	Greek	Slimy
Necto	Greek	Swimming
Neo	Greek	Recent, new
Noto	Greek	Back
Occipito	Latin	Forehead
Octo	Greek	Eight
Oculo	Latin	Eye
Odon	Greek	Tooth
Omo	Greek	Shoulder
Omni	Greek	All
Onycho	Greek	Claw
Ophio	Greek	Serpent
Ornitho	Greek	Bird
Osmo	Greek	Smell
Oto	Greek	Ear
Oxy	Greek	Keen senses
Nano	Greek	Dwarf
Naso	Latin	Nose
Pachy	Greek	Thick
Patri	Greek	Father
Ped, podo	Latin, Greek	Foot
Phago	Greek	Eating
Penta	Greek	Five
Peros	Greek	Deformed
Platy	Greek	Flat, wide
Plesio	Greek	Near
Poly	Greek	Many
Proto	Greek	First
Pseudo	Greek	False
Ptero	Greek	Wing, feather
Pyro	Greek	Fire
Retro	Latin	Backward
Rhampho	Greek	Crooked beak
Rhino	Greek	Nose
Rhipi	Greek	Fan shaped
Rhodo	Greek	Red
Rhombo	Latin	Spinning
Sapro	Greek	Rotten
Sarco	Greek	Flesh
Scolo	Greek	Crooked
Scyto	Greek	Leather
Segno	Latin	Sign
Spheno	Greek	Wedge shaped
Stomato	Greek	Mouth
Tecno	Greek	Child
Tenui	Latin	Thin
Tetra	Greek	Four
Titano	Greek	Gigantic
Tri	Greek	Three
Tricho	Greek	Hair
Ultra	Latin	Beyond
Xantho	Greek	Yellow
Xeno	Greek	Strange
Xipho	Greek	Sword

SUFFIXES

Cephalic	Greek	Head
Ichthys	Greek	Fish
Gnathus	Greek	Jaw
Mimus	Latin	Imitator
Nychus	Greek	Claw
Odon	Greek	Tooth
Pteryx	Greek	Wing
Raptor	Latin	Thief
Saurus	Greek	Lizard
Spinax	Latin	Spine, thorn
Spondylus	Greek	Vertebra

Name Your Friends. People often say that pets resemble their owners, but have you ever noticed how much some of your friends resemble certain dinosaurs? Everybody knows a *Pachycephalosaurus* or two. Try using dinosaurese to name your friends. Who knows, the name might stick! But be kind, because your friends get to name you too.

Can you say *Parasaurolophus* three times ... fast??

Muttaburrasaurus

SIZE: 23 feet long, 10 feet high at hips
MEANING OF NAME: Lizard from Muttaburra (a town in Australia)
TIME PERIOD: Early Cretaceous
CLASSIFICATION: Ornithischian, ornithopod, iguanodontid
LIFESTYLE: Plant eater often found in marshy areas
NOTES: Scientists are intrigued by the large bump on its nose
DISCOVERY SITE: Queensland, Australia

Hometown Dinosaurs. Sometimes dinosaurs are named for the place where they were found. For example, *Tsintaosaurus* was found in China, and *Edmontosaurus* was found near the Canadian city of Edmonton. Other times, they may be named for the scientist who found them—*Lambeosaurus*, or "Lambe's lizard," was named for a famous Canadian paleontologist.

Design a dinosaur that you would like to have named after you or named for your hometown. Explain how your dinosaur adapted to its environment. Here's an example: I grew up in a small town in the redwoods of northern California called Scotia. Because the redwoods existed when dinosaurs were around, a *Scotiasaurus* might be small and specially adapted to climb in giant trees. It could also have a beak like a woodpecker for carving a home in the trees. Because it's dark in the forest, it would need insulation to stay warm, so I'll give it feathers.

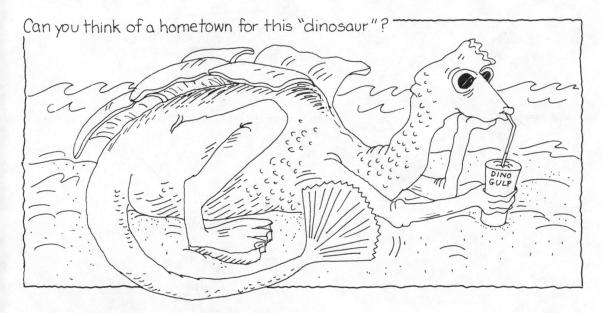

Can you think of a hometown for this "dinosaur"?

Give My Regards to Brontosaurus

You've probably heard about *Brontosaurus* (thunder lizard) since you were a little kid. After all, this 70-foot-long plant eater is one of the most famous of the dinosaurs. Now, suddenly, people are calling it *Apatosaurus* (deceptive lizard). Why?

Here's the story. In 1879 Othniel Marsh, a famous paleontologist working at Yale University, received a shipment of fossils from Colorado. With great excitement, he realized that they belonged to the largest dinosaur ever found to that point. He wrote a paper describing the fossils and called the animal *Brontosaurus*.

What Marsh didn't realize was that he had already discovered *Brontosaurus*. Two years earlier, in 1877, he had described a slightly smaller dinosaur and had called it *Apatosaurus*. Today, a century later, paleontologists have determined that the two sets of fossils actually belonged to the same type of dinosaur.

Scientists have very strict rules for naming animals. One of the rules is that the name assigned first is the one that should be used. Because the dinosaur was called *Apatosaurus* before it was called *Brontosaurus*, *Apatosaurus* is the animal's official name.

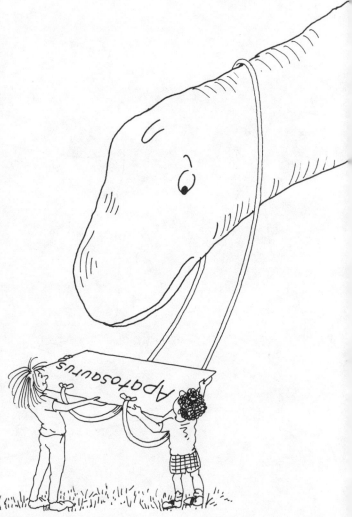

45

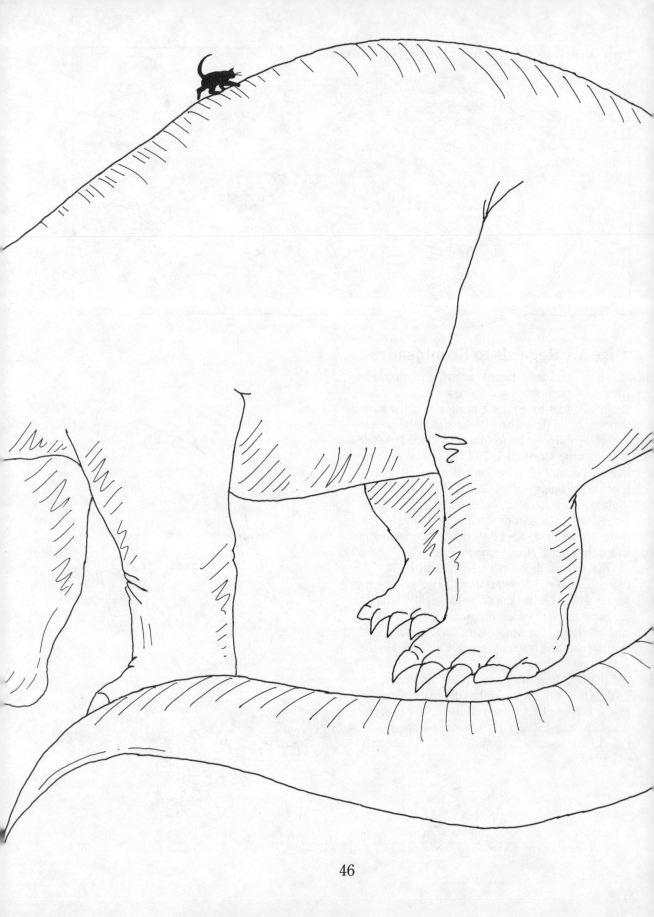

CHAPTER

3

THE CLUES TO USE

Any good detective will tell you that the best way to solve a mystery is to get on the trail while the clues are still warm. Unfortunately for paleontologists, the secrets of the dinosaurs will be discovered only by sorting through clues that are at least 65 million years old. That's what makes dinosaur hunting so challenging.

Piecing together a bunch of old, broken fossils to see the shape of an ancient animal's skeleton is tough enough, but trying to guess from those same bones what the animal really looked like, and how it acted, is even tougher. Let's look at the kinds of clues paleontologists use as they work to solve the mysteries of the dinosaurs.

Boning Up

Bones are what everybody thinks of when they hear the word *fossil*—great fossilized bones that weigh hundreds of pounds and are as long as a human being is tall. After all, these are the building blocks for those impressive skeletons we see in museums all over the world. But what is a fossilized bone? Is it bone or is it rock? And how do bones become fossilized?

Rethinking Your Bones. Most of us think of our bones as solid supports that hold up the rest of our body, nothing more than a framework to hang things on. But before we can understand how fossils are formed, we need to think about bones again.

You see, most bones are not solid. In fact, they're porous—liquids and blood pass through them all the time. The centers of some bones are filled with blood vessels, or bone marrow (where red blood cells are produced). Some animals have

bones that are hollow. If a bone is severely injured, it can die.

Bones grow and shrink, depending upon the demands placed upon them. If you increase the stress placed on a bone through exercise or work, it gradually grows thicker to handle this added work. If you reduce the stress, the bone slowly gets thinner.

Bones are made up of two main things—apatite and collagen. Apatite is a mineral. It makes bone hard. Collagen is a protein. It makes bone resilient. Take away either of these two things, and the bone changes dramatically. Read on to see how.

47

Rubber Bones. The next time your family has chicken for dinner, save some of the drumsticks (the long legbones). Clean the bones by boiling them in water. Scrub off all the meat and cartilage with an old toothbrush and soapy water.

Place the bone in a container filled with vinegar and cover it to keep the smell of the vinegar from filling the house. Leave the bone in the vinegar for three to four days.

When you take the bone out, what has happened to it? It now bends as if it were made of rubber! Try tying it in a knot. The vinegar has dissolved the apatite (the mineral in the bone), leaving only collagen. Because collagen is soft and rubbery, you can literally bend the old bone any way you like.

The next question is, what happens when you break down the collagen in a bone? Try the following experiment to find out.

Brittle Bones. You'll need some clean chicken bones (not the ones you used in the previous activity). You'll also need a warm place. The oven of a gas stove that's heated by a pilot light will work. Or a spot near the furnace or heater in your home. Another possibility is near a fireplace or wood stove if your family uses it a lot.

clean, boiled bone   foil

Wrap the clean bone in a piece of aluminum foil and place it in one of these warm places. After about a week, take it out and unwrap it. You might notice that it's a bit lighter. You will also notice that it is brittle. If you hit it with a hammer, it will shatter. The bone is brittle because the heat has broken down the collagen, the rubbery protein, in the bone and left only the mineral apatite, which is brittle. This brings us back to fossil bones.

Mineral or Bone? Breaking down the collagen is the first step in the fossilization of a dead animal's bones. Once the collagen is broken down, water seeps through the bone, slowly depositing minerals from the ground. Over thousands of years, these minerals gradually replace the original bone. So fossils are actually mineral deposits within the framework of the old bone.

For fossilization to occur, a bone must remain buried for a long time. If it is uncovered after the collagen is broken down, the hot sun and winter storms will break it down very quickly.

Will Your Bones Turn to Stone? Think for a moment about how many animals are living on the earth right now. Then add to this all the animals that have lived (and died) in the 4.6-billion-year history of the planet. Whatever the number, it must be tremendously large. But with all the animals that have lived and died, why are fossils so hard to find?

Fossil bones are rare because the conditions that lead to their fossilization must be almost perfect. And the chances that a fossil will be found after it has been preserved are even rarer.

1. Animals die.

2. Scavengers feed on the bodies, crushing small bones and scattering the rest.

3. The hot sun breaks down the collagen. Most of the bones become brittle and disintegrate in the weather.

4. Only those bones that are buried quickly survive. Here the few bones that fell in the stream have been buried in sand. In some low-lying areas, such as a swamp, a rapid burial is more likely to occur.

5. The bone must remain buried for a long time while it is slowly fossilized. During this time it is subject to great pressures that might crush it.

6. Once the bone is fossilized, it must work its way back up to the surface from under the tons of rock that lie above it. This is done through uplift or erosion, which expose the fossil-bearing rocks.

7. Once uncovered, the bone must be found before it is broken up by the weather; that is, someone must happen by the spot before the fossil is broken up by the wind and rain and snow.

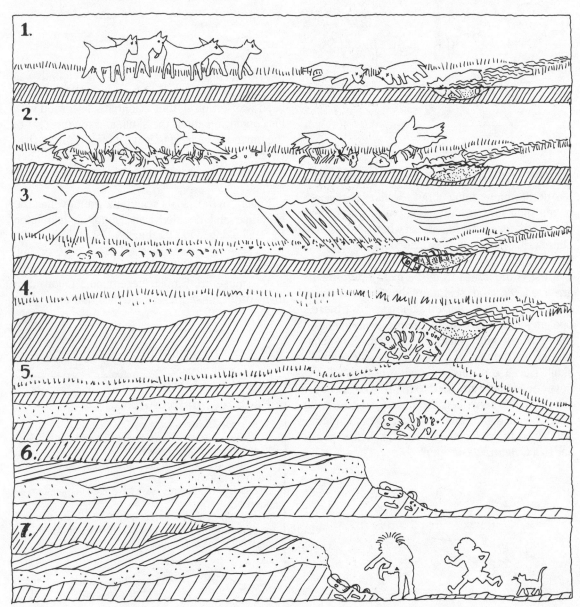

49

Few bones make it through this perilous trip. That's why fossils are so rare. One scientist estimated that less than one-tenth of one percent of the animals that have lived on the earth leave fossil remains. So your chances of becoming a fossil and having your skeleton appear in a museum in the distant future are not too good. (Unless you move to a swamp. Then they'll improve a bit!)

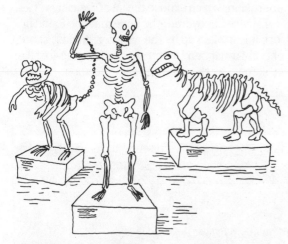

How Apatosaurus Lost Its Head

Another funny thing about fossils is that some bones show up more often as fossils than others do. Teeth, for example, are very hard and survive quite well. Smaller, more fragile bones usually get broken up.

Most of the bones from the giant *Apatosaurus* are massive, and scientists have found many almost-complete fossilized skeletons. But there's one important part of an *Apatosaurus* skeleton that is fragile and usually gets smashed or separated from the rest of the skeleton—the animal's skull. Because of this, an *Apatosaurus* skull has never been found attached to the rest of the body. When Marsh described the first *Apatosaurus* in 1883, he put a skull on it that had been found four miles from the rest of the body. The skull was similar to a *Camarasaurus* skull.

Then in 1909 Earl Douglass of Pittsburgh's Carnegie Museum found an almost-complete *Apatosaurus* at what is today called Dinosaur National Monument. One of the missing parts was the skull, but 12 feet away from the last vertebra, in the same stratum, he found a skull that matched perfectly. It was much different from the one Marsh had given to his *Apatosaurus*. It looked like this:

The skeleton that Douglass had found was mounted in the Carnegie Museum in 1915, but the head was left off. Other scientists disagreed with his conclusion about the skull, and the director of the museum decided to leave it off. For more than twenty years the *Apatosaurus* had no head. Then a cast of a *Camarasaurus* head was placed on the animal.

Finally, in the 1970s scientists went over all the evidence and decided that Douglass had been right all along. On October 20, 1979, exactly 70 years after its discovery, the *Camarasaurus* skull was replaced with the correct one in a ceremony at the museum. Similar ceremonies followed in many other museums around the country.

Pachycephalosaurus

SIZE: Up to 26 feet long
MEANING OF NAME: Thick-headed lizard
TIME PERIOD: Late Cretaceous
CLASSIFICATION: Ornithischian, ornithopod, pachycephalosaur
LIFESTYLE: Plant eater; may have lived in mountainous areas
NOTES: Thick skull was probably used to establish position within herd, as in modern mountain sheep
DISCOVERY SITE: Montana, U.S.A.

Bone Crazy

There's something about giant dinosaur bones that drives even great scientists a little bit crazy. Over the years there have been several "fossil wars" where paleontologists competed with each other to find the best specimens.

The most famous of these "wars" occurred in the 1800s between two of the great American paleontologists, O. C. Marsh and E. D. Cope. Between them these two men were responsible for identifying hundreds of new dinosaurs, including many of the most famous. Throughout their careers, however, they were enemies. They secretly sent out rival crews to find the best fossil locations, spied on each other's work, and even destroyed fossils so that their "enemies" wouldn't find them. Bill Reed, one of Marsh's best collectors, described an encounter with a rival crew in this letter to his boss (punctuation has been added):

"I went down [to the quarry] the next morning and got there as soon as they did. . . . I asked them what they were going to do. They said, dig for bones. I told them they could not get any bones there. They said they would see.

"I went to the top of the back wall with a pick and commenced to let down dirt and rocks. They told me to leave, but I was not quite ready to go. And I stayed with them for four days. I have got a big pile of dirt in that hole in the ground, more I think than they wil[l] want to dig out at any rate. I can get there before they get into where there are any bones. They are doing lots of talking down at the Station [the railway station where Cope's crew was based], but that does not hurt me nor scare me much either."

At another time, Reed reported that he had "taken the liberty to demolish to the best of my ability [all remaining bones] because there are other parties in the field collecting."

Those were the days when paleontology was a rough-and-tumble business. Even today, tempers can get pretty hot when paleontologists gather to talk about some of the more controversial theories about dinosaurs.

Under Your Nose!

Everybody knows whose picture is on a five-dollar bill, right? Abraham Lincoln. But have you ever looked closely to see what else is on a five-dollar bill? I mean *really* close—with a magnifying lens. If you do, you'll find something surprising.

Go ahead, try it. Borrow a five-dollar bill from your mom or dad and look at the picture of the Lincoln Memorial with a magnifier. Do you see any names written on the building? It may take a while to find them. Keep looking.

In all, there are 26 names written there. Can you read them? Write them on a sheet of paper. Do you have any idea why those names are there? No, the names don't belong to President Lincoln's favorite dinosaurs. This is just to show you that you don't have to look very far to find interesting things. Sometimes they're right under your nose!

Something similar happened to the paleontologists who first hunted fossils in the western United States. They were so excited at finding giant dinosaur bones that they literally walked over another kind of fossil that was right under their noses.

What they didn't notice were the microvertebrate fossils. As their name suggests, they come from very small (micro) animals with a backbone (vertebrate). They ranged from tiny lizard jaws and fish scales to baby dinosaur bones and mammal teeth. Dinosaurs may have been the most impressive animals that lived on the earth during the Mesozoic, but they were by no means the only ones. In fact, some of the tiny mammals that scurried around under the dinosaurs' feet are your distant ancestors.

Microfossils have become more and more important to paleontologists as they attempt to reconstruct the community of animals that were around when the dinosaurs were alive. How did these small animals live? And why did many of them survive when the dinosaurs suddenly disappeared? Let's take a look at some of the things microfossils can tell us.

On Your Nose! Paleontologists long overlooked these fossils simply because they were so small. To see them you have to get down on hands and knees, put your nose to the ground, and look really hard. It's dirty, time-consuming work, but it's also rewarding because it helps build a picture of the dinosaur's total environment.

We've created a microfossil hunting ground on the opposite page to give you some idea of what it takes to find and identify microfossils. All you'll need to explore it is a hand lens, one of about 8 power or so.

Look through the fossils carefully, using the key on the page to identify what you find. Record the types of fossils you find on a piece of paper and keep track of how many of each kind there are. Once you've collected the data, we'll try to draw some conclusions about what this area was like when these creatures were alive.

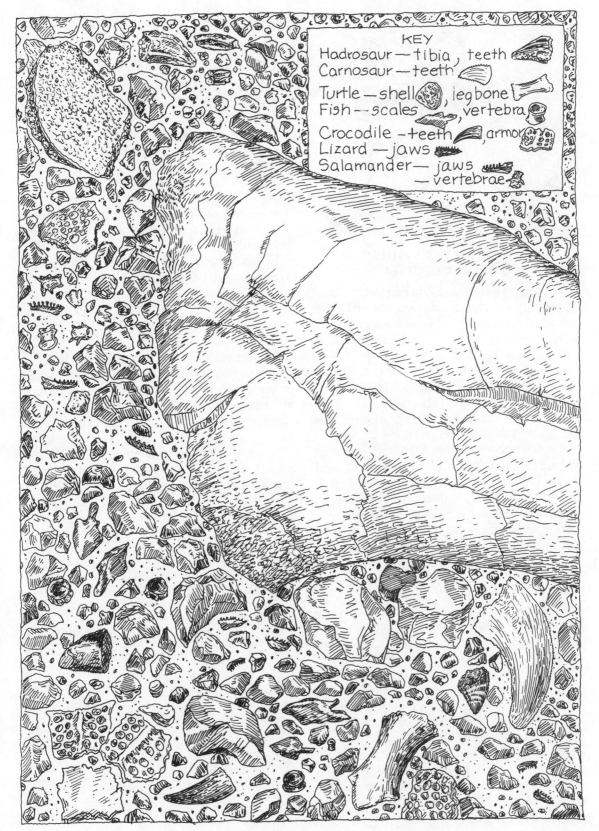

KEY
Hadrosaur — tibia , teeth
Carnosaur — teeth
Turtle — shell , leg bone
Fish — scales , vertebra
Crocodile — teeth , armor
Lizard — jaws
Salamander — jaws
— vertebrae

J. B. Hatcher's Antsy Paleontologists

The year was 1889, and John Bell Hatcher must have been frustrated. He had established himself as one of the world's best fossil hunters. In fact, he had discovered the first of the ceratopsian dinosaurs, including the mighty *Triceratops*. But the finds that made his boss, Professor O. C. Marsh, most excited were tiny mammal fossils, which were also from the late Cretaceous period.

"Put more effort into finding the mammal teeth," Marsh's letter had urged.

Hatcher knew that mammal fossils were rare and very difficult to find. One entire day of hard, painstaking work might yield only two tiny teeth. Then one day, Hatcher discovered a secret. He found special areas where small fossils were very numerous. Using his new trick, he was able to collect as many as 87 mammal fossils in a single day. Before the end of the summer he had shipped more than 800 fossil teeth to his boss in New Haven.

Other paleontologists were puzzled by his sudden success. Nobody could figure out how he did it. Years later Hatcher revealed his secret—ants. He wrote: ". . . the ant hills, which in this region are quite numerous, should be carefully inspected, as they will almost always yield a goodly number of mammal teeth. It is well to be provided with a small flour sifter with which to sift the sand contained in these ant-hills, thus freeing it of finer materials and subjecting the coarser material remaining in the sieve to a thorough inspection for mammals. By this method, the writer has frequently secured 200 to 300 teeth and jaws from one ant-hill."

As the ants dig their homes, they uncover the small bones, which they carry to the surface and arrange around the openings in the hill. Nobody knows why they do this. Some think that the fossils serve as heat collectors that help to keep the colony warm. But to Hatcher the ant's habit was a great help.

With the ants doing most of the heavy work of uncovering and gathering the fossils, Hatcher just sifted through the dirt on top of the anthills with an old flour sifter. That way, he could keep Marsh happy with a steady supply of microvertebrate fossils and still have time to pursue the more glamorous ceratopsian dinosaurs that were his first love.

In 1893, frustrated in his search for mammal fossils in an area without anthills, Hatcher decided to bring in some reinforcements. He brought in a few shovelfuls of sand from a distant hill. When he returned two years later, he found 33 mammal teeth. The ants had done their work.

Modern paleontologists have refined Hatcher's technique, using it to find tens of thousands of microvertebrate fossils. When they find an area rich in these fossils, they dig up the dirt with shovels and place it in specially built boxes with bottoms made of fine wire mesh. Then they set the boxes in the nearest lake or stream and leave them there for a few days. When they return, the dirt is washed away, and only small rocks and fossils remain. These are then taken back to the laboratory to be studied.

Saltasaurus

SIZE: 40 feet long
MEANING OF NAME: Lizard from Salta (a province of Argentina)
TIME PERIOD: Late Cretaceous
CLASSIFICATION: Saurischian, sauropodamorph, sauropod, titanosaurid
LIFESTYLE: Flexible tail indicated it may have reared up on its back legs to reach leaves in tallest trees
NOTES: It is the first armored sauropod; hundreds of bony studs covered its back and sides
DISCOVERY SITE: Salta, Argentina

Carbon Copies

The most beautiful fossils are not necessarily the largest. In fact, quite the opposite. Under the right conditions thin, delicate leaves can be preserved in perfect detail as a carbon film printed on the rocks. The carbon for the copy is produced as the organic matter in the leaves decays.

At the Lawrence Hall of Science in Berkeley, California, kids learn how to create their own carbon leaf prints. You can try it at home. Gather some large leaves that have interesting shapes and patterns. Then try making a carbon leaf print.

You will need:
    leaves
    a candle and matches (let a grown-up know what you're doing!)
    aluminum foil, 8 inches by 10 inches
    paper towels
    construction paper
    plastic wrap
    tweezers

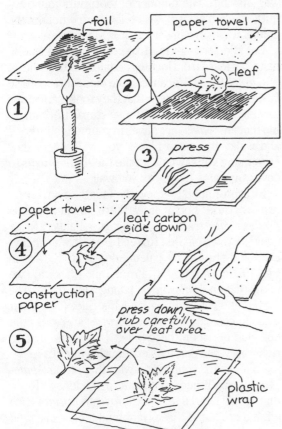

1. Clear off a wide area on a table. Light the candle.

2. Hold the aluminum foil about one inch above the candle flame. Hold it there until carbon from the flame coats the foil. Extinguish the candle.

3. Put the foil on the table, carbon side up. Place your leaf on top of the foil. Cover it with a piece of paper towel and press down firmly.

4. Remove the towel. Use the tweezers to pick up the leaf by its stem. Place the leaf carbon side down on the construction paper. Lay a clean paper towel over the leaf and press down firmly.

5. Remove the towel and leaf. If all went well, you should have a perfect copy of your leaf. To keep the carbon from smudging, cover your print with a piece of plastic wrap.

"Ick Nology" Illustrated

Some of the most valuable fossils are really nothing at all. Just holes or impressions left behind by an animal taking a stroll across a soft muddy beach. Fortunately for us, some of these holes have been preserved when the mud hardened into stone.

Fossils that don't actually include any part of the animal, but contain evidence that the animal was there, are called *trace fossils*. They include skin impressions and nests. The most common dinosaur trace fossils, however, are footprints.

Single dinosaur footprints are useful, but it's even better when the prints are found in groups that form a *trackway*. These trackways can sometimes be even more valuable than fossilized bones. After all, a bone doesn't become fossilized until after an animal dies, while trackways were made when the animal was still alive and going about its daily business.

Paleontologists who study footprints are called *ichnologists* (ick nologists). They are specialists in finding out as much as possible from the footprints. The depth of a print, for example, can tell them how heavy a dinosaur was or what kind of ground it was walking over. The distance between each footprint may tell them how fast the dinosaur

was moving. The number of footprints found together in a trackway also tells them whether the animal was traveling alone or in a herd.

Let's look at some of the things that ichnologists can learn from looking at dinosaur footprints.

Giant Strides. Because some dinosaurs were so large, it stands to reason that they took giant steps as well. But how big were those steps? Let's imagine that an *Apatosaurus* lives in your neighborhood and walks the same places you walk every day. How many steps would it take the *Apatosaurus* to cover the same distances you walk?

First, we need to know the length of an *Apatosaurus* stride. Fortunately, there's a very famous *Apatosaurus* trackway along the Paluxy River near the town of Glen Rose, Texas. It was uncovered and studied by paleontologist R. T. Bird in the 1930s and 1940s. From this trackway we know that an *Apatosaurus* taking a leisurely stroll moved about 13 feet with each stride. (Note that a stride consists of two *consecutive* steps. So the distance between the two left footprints (or two right ones, for that matter) equals your stride.

To compare your stride with that of the *Apatosaurus*, you'll need to create a trackway. To do that, you'll need five *Apatosaurus* footprints (two left hind feet and three right hind feet) and a tape measure or yardstick. Use the pattern below to

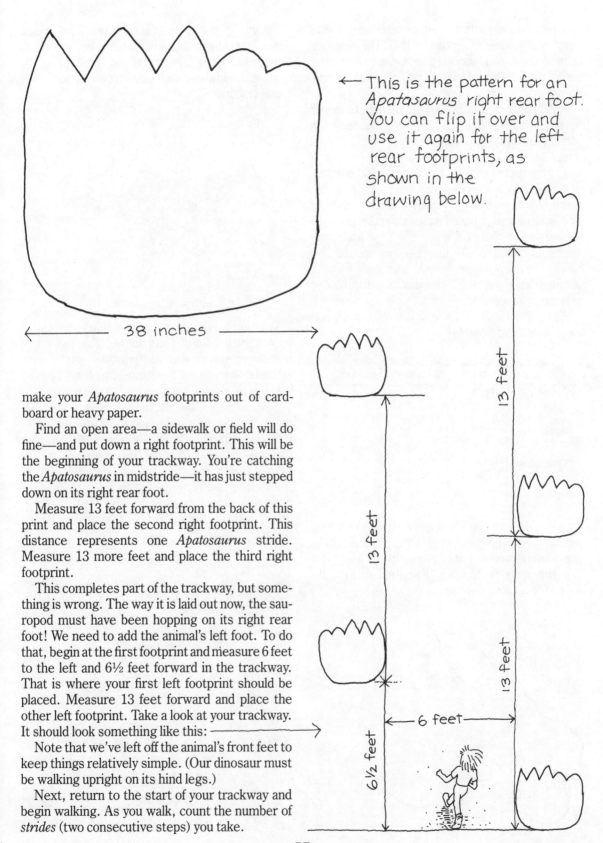

← This is the pattern for an *Apatasaurus* right rear foot. You can flip it over and use it again for the left rear footprints, as shown in the drawing below.

← 38 inches →

13 feet

13 feet

13 feet

6 feet

6½ feet

make your *Apatosaurus* footprints out of cardboard or heavy paper.

Find an open area—a sidewalk or field will do fine—and put down a right footprint. This will be the beginning of your trackway. You're catching the *Apatosaurus* in midstride—it has just stepped down on its right rear foot.

Measure 13 feet forward from the back of this print and place the second right footprint. This distance represents one *Apatosaurus* stride. Measure 13 more feet and place the third right footprint.

This completes part of the trackway, but something is wrong. The way it is laid out now, the sauropod must have been hopping on its right rear foot! We need to add the animal's left foot. To do that, begin at the first footprint and measure 6 feet to the left and 6½ feet forward in the trackway. That is where your first left footprint should be placed. Measure 13 feet forward and place the other left footprint. Take a look at your trackway. It should look something like this: ─────→

Note that we've left off the animal's front feet to keep things relatively simple. (Our dinosaur must be walking upright on its hind legs.)

Next, return to the start of your trackway and begin walking. As you walk, count the number of *strides* (two consecutive steps) you take.

57

When you reach the end of the trackway, divide your total number of strides by two. This number tells you how many strides it took you to move the same distance an *Apatosaurus* covered in one stride.

Let's say that it took you 22 strides to cover your trackway. This means that you took 11 strides for each *Apatosaurus* stride. We'll call 11 your "*Apatosaurus* quotient."

For the rest of the day, try counting the number of strides it takes to get to different places, divide this number by your *Apatosaurus* quotient and see how many steps it would have taken the giant dinosaur to get there. You can use practically any destination near your house—the end of the block, the store, your school, your best friend's house—but don't make the distance too far, or you might lose count!

Keep a data sheet on your travels. It should look something like this:

DESTINATION	NUMBER OF STRIDES	APATASAURUS QUOTIENT	APATASAURUS STRIDES
school	451	11	41
park			
Dave's house			
store			

If you'd like to see how your stride stacks up against one of the giant carnosaurs, just substitute the *Tyrannosaurus's* stride length (12 feet) and use the same techniques described earlier. Its footprints looked like this:

Or you might try comparing the carnosaur's stride length with those of its prey. For example, *Lambeosaurus*, a late Cretaceous duck-billed dinosaur moved about six feet with each stride when it was walking.

With such a disadvantage in stride length, how do you think a *Lambeosaurus* was able to escape from meat eaters such as *Tyrannosaurus*? Later in this book you'll see how some dinosaurs evolved ways to take longer strides and to run faster.

The Missing Clue. In the last few years, pictures of dinosaurs in books and museums have changed dramatically. Trackways were one clue that led scientists to make this change. It wasn't so much that paleontologists saw something in the tracks they hadn't seen before. It's that they noticed that something was missing. What kind of tracks would you expect this animal to leave behind?

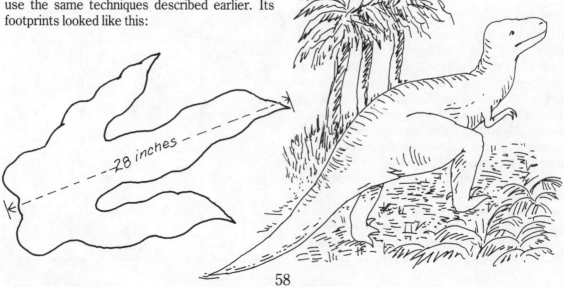

28 inches

What would it leave behind besides prints of its feet? Tail prints! If dinosaurs dragged their tails along behind them, there should be a long narrow groove in the ground between their footprints, but paleontologists seldom find any tail prints.

This observation, combined with new studies of dinosaur skeletons, led scientists to redraw many dinosaurs. The "new" dinosaurs carried their tails straight out behind their bodies. By keeping their tails high off the ground, dinosaurs were well balanced and could run fast.

What Happened Here? When paleontologist R. T. Bird and his crew began uncovering the dinosaur trackway near Glen Rose in 1939, they found that a herd of 23 *Apatosaurus* had passed through the area. The footprints showed that the animals were all sizes, both youngsters and full-grown adults. They also discovered that giant meat-eating dinosaurs had passed through the area both before and after the *Apatosaurus* herd.

Two sets of footprints seemed to tell an especially exciting story. First, the crews found the tracks of an *Apatosaurus* ambling slowly along the riverbed. Following just behind it were the three-toed footprints of a carnivore. When the *Apatosaurus* turned left, the carnivore followed.

Here was a once-in-a-lifetime chance to see these prehistoric beasts in action. The crew uncovered each new footprint with growing excitement. Was the carnosaur really stalking the sauropod? And how would the chase end? Would they come upon the dead sauropod's fossilized bones in the next few steps? Or did it escape?

Unfortunately, the end of the story remains in doubt. The footprints of the two animals disappeared beneath a limestone rock wall where the workers couldn't follow them. This story shows why dinosaur trackways are so exciting. We may never know what happened to the *Apatosaurus* that day, or even whether the two sets of prints were made on the same day, but such "stories in stone" leave a lot of room for the imagination.

Here are some imaginary scenes captured in footprints. The dinosaurs in each scene are noted at the top of each puzzle. In each case, do some research to find out which period we're examining (Triassic, Jurassic, or Cretaceous) and try to decipher the meaning of the prints.

2. DEINONYCHOS AND TENONTOSAURUS

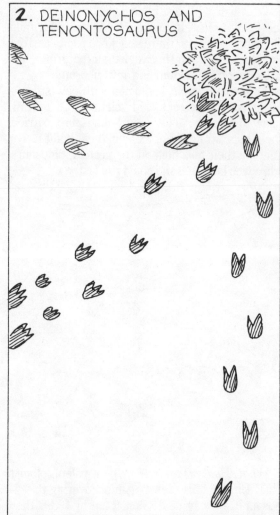

1. APATOSAURUS

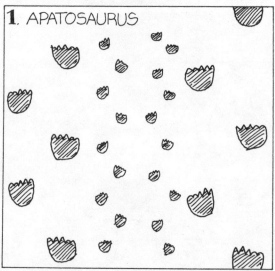

3. LAMBEOSAURS AND TYRANNOSAURUS

Old lake bed

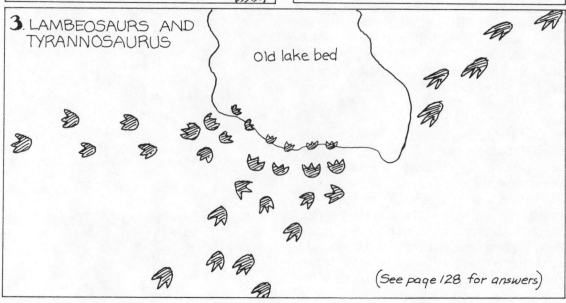

(See page 128 for answers)

Print Your Way into Prehistory. Did you have any luck deciphering the footprint puzzles? You can create your own prehistoric scenes. **You will need:**

a big sheet of paper
a ballpoint pen
a couple of large potatoes
a small paring knife
a stamp pad

1. Slice your potato in half and blot it dry on a paper towel.

2. Draw a dinosaur footprint on the flat side of the potato with the pen. Use the prints from the previous activity as a pattern.

3. Carefully carve away the excess part of the potato with the knife (ask a grown-up to help if you aren't used to working with a knife). Your "footprint" should stand at least ¼ inch above the rest of the potato.

4. Now just stamp out a scene. You might do chase scenes or fights, or try to capture a whole herd of different-size sauropods tramping through the woods. Be sure that all of the dinosaurs in your scene lived during the same time period.

A Change of Pace. Want to get your feet wet in paleontology? You'll have to if you want to try this next experiment. (If you don't want to get your feet wet, you could take a field trip to a nearby beach or river bar, or any place that's sandy. You'll probably get your feet wet there too, but it's a good excuse to go swimming!)

Remember when you compared the stride length of a *Tyrannosaurus* with that of a *Lambeosaurus*? Since *Tyrannosaurus* could move almost twice as far as *Lambeosaurus* with each stride, we wondered how the *Lambeosaurus* could ever escape. Now you'll try to find out.

To investigate this question, you'll create a trackway of a young *Homo sapiens* (humans) and see what the tracks tell us. **You will need:**

a pencil and paper to record data
a measuring device (yardstick or tape measure)
a "feet wetter," better known as a sprinkler or pail of water

Find a clean sidewalk or a paved playground and try this experiment only on a warm day (so you don't catch pneumonia). If you live near a beach or will be visiting one soon, you're in luck. Wet sand is the perfect place to make a trackway.

Parasaurolophus

First, mark off an area about the length of two *Apatosaurus* strides (26 feet). If you still have your trackway from the previous activity, it will do fine.

Take off your shoes, get your feet wet, and walk normally along the trackway. Look back at your footprints. They probably look something like this:

Measure the distance of your stride (from the rear of one print to the rear of the next same footprint) and sketch a picture of your print.

Hop in your "feet wetter" again. This time, try running as fast as you can along the trackway. Repeat your observations by measuring the length of your stride and sketching a picture of the shape of your footprint.

What differences do you notice in the two kinds of footprints? In the shape of the footprints? In the length of the stride? If you are working on a beach, notice which prints are deeper.

26 feet

You don't always make the same kind of tracks. When you are walking, almost all of the sole of your foot touches the ground. This kind of walking is called *plantigrade*. When you run, however, only the front portion of your foot touches the ground. This is called *digitigrade* walking.

An animal's speed is largely determined by the length of its legs, especially its lower legs. When an animal runs on its toes (digitigrade), it adds an additional length to its lower leg (the length of its rear footbones, or metatarsals). This lengthens the animal's stride tremendously.

Animals such as *Lambeosaurus*, which relied on speed to escape being eaten, had to move very fast if they were to survive. So over thousands of years their metatarsals became longer and longer.

Horses are a good modern example of this kind of evolution. If you compare your leg and foot-bones to the same bones on a horse, you'll see that a horse is running essentially on a single toenail all the time! Scientists call this *unguligrade* walking. Can you run on a toenail? Probably not, but I'll bet you can shift into digitigrade pretty fast when you're trying to escape the town bully!

Lambeosaurus

SIZE: Up to 33 feet long
MEANING OF NAME: Lambe's lizard (for a Canadian paleontologist)
TIME PERIOD: Late Cretaceous
CLASSIFICATION: Ornithischian, ornithopod, hadrosaurid
LIFESTYLE: A plant eater that lived in herds on low-land plains
NOTES: Grazed on four legs until frightened, when it fled on two legs
DISCOVERY SITE: Alberta, Canada

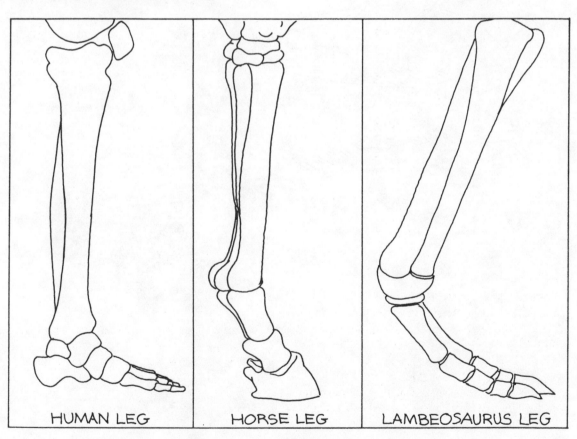

HUMAN LEG   HORSE LEG   LAMBEOSAURUS LEG

63

Bring 'em Back in Plaster

Imagine making your very own cast of a 185,000,000-year-old dinosaur footprint and bringing it home to display in your room! You can do just that if you live in the northeastern United States or if your family plans to visit that area soon. The place to go is Dinosaur State Park in Hartford, Connecticut. And when you visit there, take along a lot of plaster of paris.

Dinosaur State Park includes a trackway that has hundreds of dinosaur footprints. It was discovered in the 1960s by workers clearing ground for a new state building. The three-toed footprints ranged from 10 to 16 inches in length and were probably made by a creature much like *Dilopho-saurus*, a meat-eating dinosaur from the Jurassic period.

The state preserved the area as a park, and they've covered parts of the trackway with a 122-foot geodesic dome to protect it. It's a fascinating exhibit, but what's even better is that they've set aside an outdoor casting area for visitors.

According to the rangers, all you need is to bring along 10 pounds of plaster of paris (15 for the biggest footprints), some old rags, ¼ cup cooking oil, and a putty knife or table knife. You'll need water too (3 to 4½ quarts), but you can get that at the park. Full directions for making a print are available at the park. If you need more information, the phone number is (203) 529–8423.

Cast away!

CHAPTER

4

DINOSAUR CONSTRUCTION ZONE

For paleontologists the fun really begins once a dinosaur's bones have been dug up and brought back to the lab for cleaning. That's when they try to put the whole thing together and see what it has to say for itself.

Fortunately, paleontologists have patterns—modern animals—to follow when they try to piece these puzzles back together. All vertebrates (animals with backbones), whether a giant elephant or your family cat, are built from the same basic blueprint.

at the pelvis. Add the ribs and a few extra bones to protect the animal's soft organs and you're done.

This same pattern is followed in all living vertebrates. Try to find bones in these skeletons that match those in the cat's skeleton.

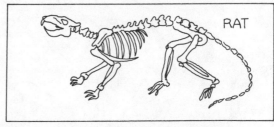

RAT

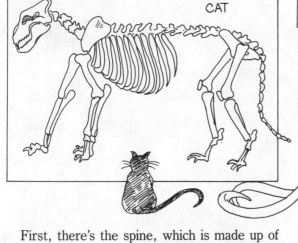

CAT

ELEPHANT

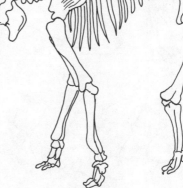

First, there's the spine, which is made up of pieces called *vertebrae*. The head, or skull, goes on one end, while the other end becomes the tail. The spine is supported by two pairs of legs. The forelegs in front and the rear legs, which connect

65

CHAPTER

4

DINOSAUR CONSTRUCTION ZONE

For paleontologists the fun really begins once a dinosaur's bones have been dug up and brought back to the lab for cleaning. That's when they try to put the whole thing together and see what it has to say for itself.

Fortunately, paleontologists have patterns—modern animals—to follow when they try to piece these puzzles back together. All vertebrates (animals with backbones), whether a giant elephant or your family cat, are built from the same basic blueprint.

at the pelvis. Add the ribs and a few extra bones to protect the animal's soft organs and you're done.

This same pattern is followed in all living vertebrates. Try to find bones in these skeletons that match those in the cat's skeleton.

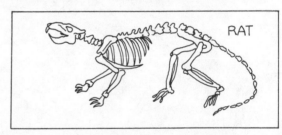

RAT

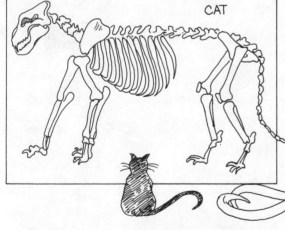

CAT

ELEPHANT

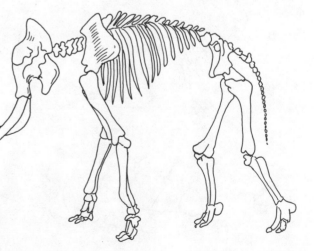

First, there's the spine, which is made up of pieces called *vertebrae*. The head, or skull, goes on one end, while the other end becomes the tail. The spine is supported by two pairs of legs. The forelegs in front and the rear legs, which connect

Dinosaur Puzzlers

Paleontologists use the blueprints provided by modern animals as clues to help them reassemble dinosaur skeletons. You can try the same thing. Photocopy this page and cut out each group of bones. Then use the skeleton below as a pattern to help you reassemble the entire dinosaur. First, lay the bones out on another piece of paper. Once you have them in the right place, use gluestick to hold them down.

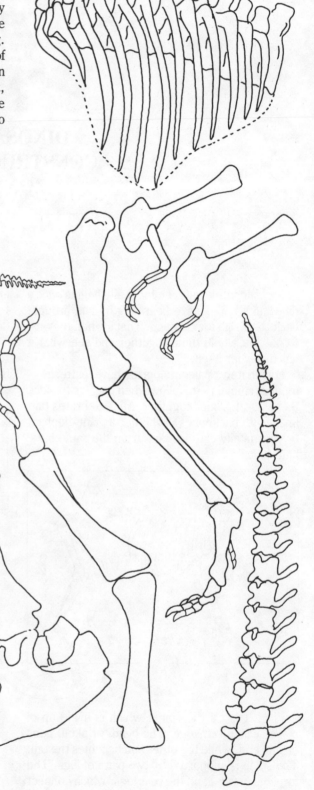

Filling in the Blanks. Unfortunately, paleontologists don't usually find all the pieces of a dinosaur's skeleton in one place. Most of the time, some of the pieces have been crushed or carried away. To fill in these blanks, they look at bones from similar skeletons.

Photocopy this page and try reassembling the skeleton. When you come upon missing bones, use the dinosaur skeleton on the previous page as a pattern for drawing in the lost pieces.

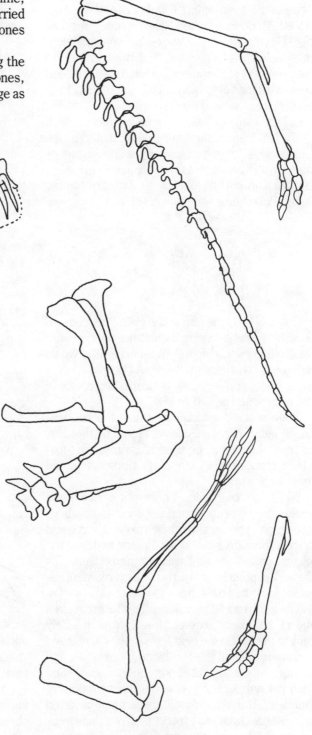

(completed on page 128)

Dinosaurs Get Plastered

The West was still wild in 1876 when E. D. Cope and his assistant, Charles Sternberg, explored Montana's Judith River country for fossils. The trip to the Far West was a long and difficult one for the collectors. And the trip back to the professor's laboratory in Philadelphia, loaded down with tons of fossils, was even rougher, both for the scientists and for their fossils.

In fact, many of the fossils never made it back to the lab. Instead they were jostled and crushed into useless fragments as they were moved by wagon over the roadless countryside to the nearest rail station then loaded into boxcars for the bumpy 1,500-mile train ride east.

One day near the end of the collecting season, Sternberg was admiring a great horned dinosaur skull the crew had found, wondering if it would survive the trip back to the lab. As he mulled over the breakage problem, he noticed a bag of rice in the wagon, and he had an idea.

None of the crew liked rice, and the bag was unopened. It may be useless as food, he thought, but perhaps it could be useful for protecting fossils. Sternberg told Cope of his brainstorm, and they set to work.

While the cook boiled a huge pot of rice into a gooey glue, Sternberg and Cope cut burlap bags into strips. They soaked the strips in the goo and draped them over the skull. Before bedtime the job was done—the skull was swathed in bandages like an Egyptian mummy. By the next morning the entire mess had hardened.

The idea worked magnificently. The great skull and all the other "jacketed" fossils made it safely back to the lab. In the next few seasons, Cope and Sternberg refined the technique (flour paste and plaster were substituted for the rice goo), and soon paleontologists everywhere were following their lead. Today, fossils still are carefully jacketed in plaster and cloth to protect them on their journey to the lab. Once they reach the laboratory, the plaster jackets are sawed open so that the fossils can be cleaned and preserved.

Sizing Up Dinosaurs

One of the first things paleontologists can usually determine from looking at a dinosaur skeleton is the animal's size. In fact, they can usually estimate size just by looking at a few bones, assuming that the missing pieces are of the same proportions.

Everyone talks about how large dinosaurs were. And it's true; some of them were quite large. *Brachiosaurus*, which lived at the end of the Jurassic period and which weighed about 85 tons, is usually thought of as the largest land animal that ever lived on the earth, while *Diplodocus*, at over 90 feet, is called the longest.

But that's not the whole story. Dinosaurs were more than just giants. They came in almost every size imaginable. Some were very small. Some were low and wide, like a tank. Others were tall and thin, like an ostrich. Let's investigate some of these fascinating dinosaur dimensions.

Newly Discovered Dinosaur Outstretches Diplodocus. Flash! A new find in New Mexico might change these records. The tail vertebrae and a partial thighbone of a new, giant sauropod have been uncovered—and there are more bones still in the ground. Dubbed *Seismosaurus* (earth-shaking lizard), it is estimated that the giant was 100 to 120 feet long and weighted 80 to 100 tons. Before it can be called the longest dinosaur, however, more of it will have to be dug up.

How Tall Were Dinosaurs?

In 1979 paleontologist Jim Jensen was prospecting in western Colorado when he discovered an amazing fossil. It was the shoulder blade (scapula) of a "new" dinosaur. That was exciting. But what made his find even more interesting was the fact that the scapula was more than 10 feet long!

To have a 10-foot scapula, the dinosaur must have stood 50 to 60 feet tall and weighed more than 80 tons. Because of the huge size of the fossil, Jensen named the new dinosaur *Ultrasaurus*.

It's hard to imagine any animal that is 60 feet tall. One good way to really understand how tall some dinosaurs were is to compare them to familiar objects around your home or school. Depending on where you live, you can compare them to things like your house, tall trees, a silo, or a tall office building.

Here's an easy way to estimate heights so you can compare them to *Ultrasaurus* and the other giant dinosaurs. All you need is a stick and one of your friends to use as a giant ruler. It's easiest if your ruler (friend) is a relatively even number in height—that is, say 4 or 4½ feet, something like that.

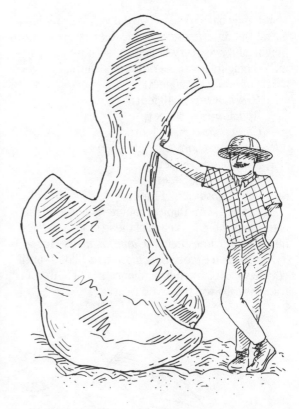

Here's how you would measure a building:

1. Have a friend stand against the building you want to measure.
Step back until you can easily see the entire building. Hold the stick upright in your outstretched hand and mark your friend's height on the stick with your thumb.

2. Count how many times this height "stacks" to reach the top of the building.

3. Now multiply the number of "stacks" by your friend's height to get the building's height.

You may have to search awhile to find anything as tall as an *Ultrasaurus* (60 feet is about the height of a five-story building), so here are estimated heights for some other dinosaurs:

Supersaurus, 50 feet;
Brachiosaurus, 40 feet;
Apatosaurus, 30 feet;
Camarasaurus, 25 feet;
Tyrannosaurus, 22 feet;
Iguanodon, 18 feet;
Allosaurus, 15 feet;
and *Stegosaurus*, 11 feet.

Try to find something in your neighborhood that is the same height as each of these dinosaurs. You might even name them—*Camarasaurus* House, *Tyrannosaurus* Tree, *Brachiosaurus* Silo, —until you have a block full of dinosaurs. Then your friends really will think you're crazy!

Try to imagine what it would be like to be 60 feet tall. You'd definitely get a different perspective on the world.

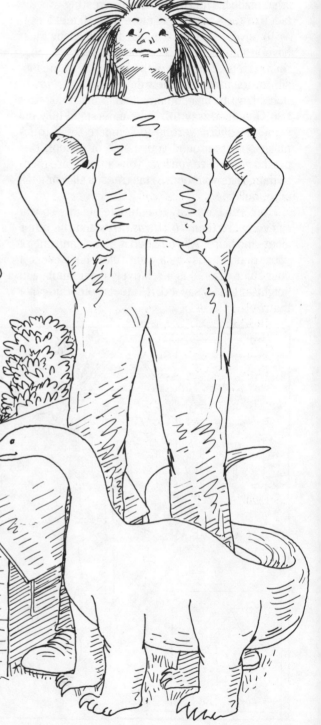

The Advantages of Being Big

There's one general rule that's true for all animals—they're exactly the right size. Think about it for a moment. Every animal, whether an ant or an *Ultrasaurus*, is the size it is for a reason. Elephants are large so that no other animal dares to attack them. Giraffes are tall so they can reach the leaves at the tops of trees. Ants are just the right size for living in colonies and feeding on small bits of food.

If this is true, then why did some of the dinosaurs grow so large? There has to be a reason. One reason seems plain. Large size is a good defense against meat-eating predators. But there's also another reason, and that's what we'll look at in the next experiment.

Water Watching. Watching water cool may not be your idea of having a good time, but comparing how fast different volumes of water lose heat will give you a good idea of why some of the dinosaurs became so large. **You will need:**

> **a thermometer that records as high as 200 degrees F.**
> **a teakettle for boiling water**
> **a clear 2-cup measuring cup that can hold very hot water**
> **permission from a grown-up to use the stove (explain that it's for science)**
> **a pad and pencil for recording data**
> **graph paper for illustrating the data**
> **a watch or clock that reads seconds**

1. First, set up your data sheet. You'll be measuring two volumes of water, so you'll need two columns. Label one column "¼ cup" and the other column "2 cups." Down the side, label the rows in minutes from 1 to 30. When you're done, the data sheet will look like this:

2. Fill the teakettle with water and heat it on the stove until it's just about to boil.

3. Place the thermometer in the measuring cup and add ¼ cup of water. Record the temperature of the water as soon as you pour it. Start your timer so you can check the temperature each minute for 30 minutes. Record the data on your sheet.

4. Empty the measuring cup and bring the water in the teakettle almost to a boil again. This time, pour 2 cups of water into the measuring cup and record the temperatures at the same time intervals as you did for the ¼ cup.

Record temperature of water each minute for 30 minutes.

minutes | ¼ cup | 2 cups

number one to 30 minutes

71

Looking At Your Data. Graphs help scientists analyze data. By converting the numbers into lines, they get a much clearer picture of what the numbers mean. Use your sheet of graph paper to set up a graph that looks like this:

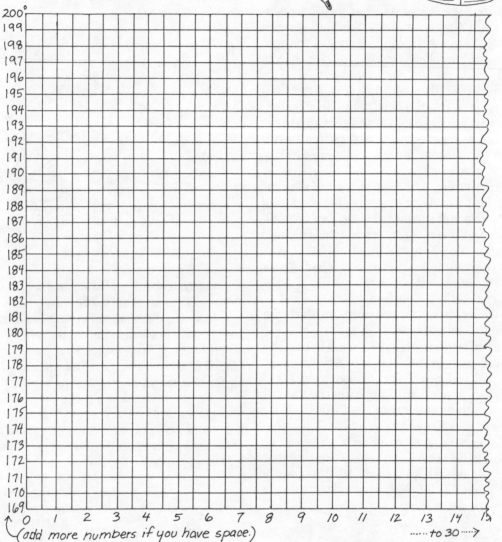

(add more numbers if you have space.) ......to 30 ....>

1. The numbers along the bottom of the graph represent the number of minutes since the water was poured. The numbers that run up the left side of the graph represent the temperature of the water.

2. Graph the ¼-cup sample first. To record a temperature, find the point where the time and temperature cross. For example, if your water was 190 degrees at the 0 minute, you'd follow the 0-minute line up until it crossed the 190-degree line. Mark that spot with a small x.

3. Next, move to the 1-minute line and follow it up to where it crosses the temperature you recorded for that time. Continue in this manner until you've recorded all your data on the chart.

4. Draw a line that connects the x's. You may want to use a ruler to make your lines straight. Label this line "¼ cup."

5. Now use the same techniques to record the data for the 2-cup sample. This time, connect the data points with a broken line. Label the broken line "2 cups."

Congratulations for completing your graph. Graphing is an important skill that scientists use all the time to analyze data. Today, many scientists have computer programs that do the graphing for them, but it's still valuable to be able to draw graphs.

Your graph now shows you how fast the two water samples cooled. Look at it carefully. Which water sample cooled faster? (The steeper the line, the faster the cooling.) Write down your observations.

We'll discuss the results and explain what this has to do with dinosaurs in a minute. But right now you have a little bit of cleaning up to do in the kitchen.

Now for the results. The smaller water sample (¼ cup) cooled much faster than the larger sample. That is because the larger sample has a much larger volume and only a slightly larger surface area than the smaller sample. Therefore it can't give off heat as fast.

(For the math fans in the audience, this rule can be shown in math terms. As an animal increases in size, its volume and weight increase in proportion to the cube of the length. Its surface area, however, increases in proportion to the square of the length.)

If you try it with larger volumes of water, say 2 gallons (or even 2,000 gallons), you'll find that the cooling rate slows even further. The temperature in large bodies of water varies much more slowly than it does in small bodies.

The same thing is true with animals. Scientists estimate that the internal temperature of a large sauropod such as *Brachiosaurus* varied no more than one degree from a warm day to a cold night. That is because the volume of its body was so large compared to its surface area.

Whereas some of the small dinosaurs may have been warm-blooded and had fur or feathers to hold in their body heat, the large dinosaurs were able to maintain a stable body temperature simply because of their great size. Even if they were cold-blooded, they didn't have to warm themselves in the sun each morning because they never got cold. This was a great advantage, so as long as their bones could support the weight, the sauropods could gradually become larger and larger.

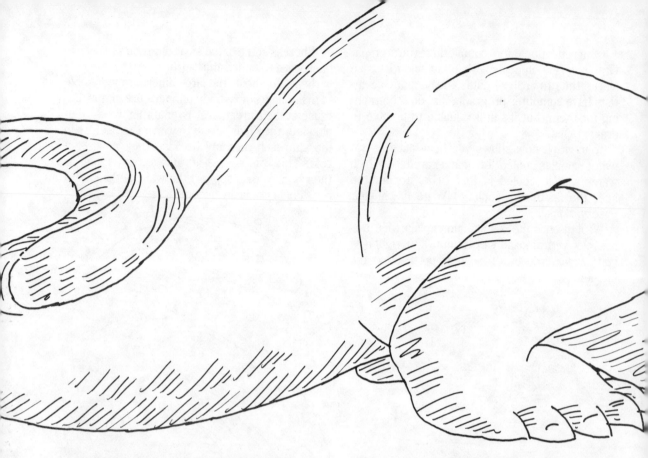

The Problems of Being Big

And that brings us to one of the problems of being big—having bones strong enough to hold up all that weight. The largest known animal on the earth is alive today. Do you know what it is? How does it support the great weight of its body?

One reason the dinosaurs were able to grow so large is that low down on their bodies, in the legs and feet, they had massive, thick bones, while their upper bodies—their skull and back vertebrae—were very lightweight. In fact, *Camarasaurus* got its name, which means "chamber lizard," because its vertebrae were hollowed out, making them as light as possible.

Camarasaurus's head, too, was designed to be as light as possible. Notice how little bone there is in the skull.

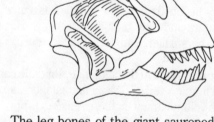

The leg bones of the giant sauropods, on the other hand, were massive, and their feet were very wide, important characteristics for supporting great weight.

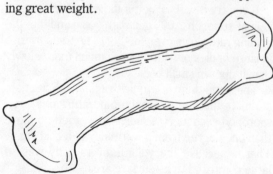

As far as we know, adult blue whales are the largest animals that have ever lived on the earth. These giant mammals can be more than 70 feet long and weigh more than 100 tons. The water they swim in supports their great weight.

74

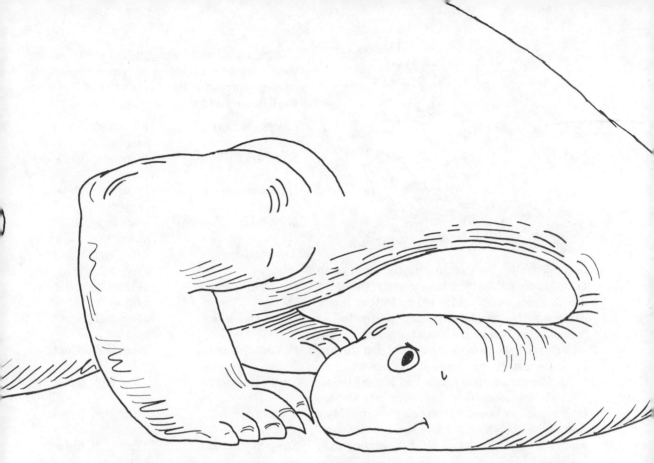

Nature is a good engineer. Supporting structures such as bones are usually no heavier than they absolutely have to be to stand up to normal wear and tear.

Dinosaur Heart Breaker. Have you ever fainted? It happens when your brain isn't receiving enough oxygen. Oxygen is transported in the blood from the lungs, so ultimately your heart is responsible for getting the oxygen up to the brain. When your brain isn't receiving enough oxygen, your body has a simple reaction. It collapses. When you're lying flat, with your brain and heart on the same level, the brain receives a great rush of oxygen, and you recover.

Now, you're only four or five feet tall. Think how hard it would be to keep blood flowing to your brain if your head were 60 feet in the air! That's what *Ultrasaurus* had to do.

Blood pressure is measured in millimeters of mercury. Humans need 120 millimeters of mercury to maintain their blood pressure. Giraffes, on the other hand, require 260 millimeters of mercury to get the blood up to their brains.

Paleontologists estimate that an *Apatosaurus* needed a pressure of 375 millimeters of mercury to get blood to its brain, while *Ultrasaurus* would require about 550 millimeters. That's more than 4½ times the pressure created by a human heart. Can you imagine how strong the animal's heart and blood vessels must have been to produce and hold such pressure?

Inflating a bicycle tire with a hand pump is a good comparison here. First, let's pump it up to 30 pounds. It's easy. You don't have to work too hard, and the tire can hold the pressure (in fact, it's soft when you squeeze it). We'll say that you are a human heart and this is how hard you have to work to get blood to your brain.

30 pounds pressure

135 pounds??

But let's imagine that you are the heart of an *Ultrasaurus* and that you have to pump the blood 4½ times as hard to get blood up to your brain. This means that you have to inflate the tire to 135 pounds. *Don't try it!* It's almost impossible. Not only do you have to work really hard, but the tire has to be very strong to hold all the pressure.

An *Ultrasaurus* must have had a good heart, and its blood vessels must have been very strong, or it would have been fainting all the time. Now that you've seen how and why some of the dinosaurs were so large, let's look at the other end of the scale.

Household Dinosaurs

A lot of people keep modern dinosaurs for pets. After all, we know that birds are the modern descendants of dinosaurs. But some of the prehistoric dinosaurs were also about the right size to be household pets.

Can you imagine how mad you'd be when your dad told you that your *Compsognathus* couldn't sleep in your bed anymore? Or how much trouble it would be trying to make sure that your *Segisaurus* ate its lizard dinners outside.

With a yardstick, you can find things around your house that are the same size as some of the smaller dinosaurs. Here are some of the sizes you'll be looking for:

Compsognathus	1 foot high, 2 feet long
Segisaurus	18 inches high, 3 feet long
Heterodontosaurus	18 inches high, 4 feet long
Micropachycephalosaur	20 inches high, 20 inches long
Archaeopteryx	2 feet high, 3 feet long
Protoceratops	2½ feet high, 6 feet long
Heterodontosaurus	3 feet high, 4 feet long
Psittacosaurus	5 feet high, 6 feet long
Struthiosaurus	3 feet high, 6 feet long
Hypsilophodon	3 feet high, 6 feet long
Stenonychosaurus	3 feet high, 6½ feet long
Velociraptor	4 feet high, 6 feet long
Deinonychus	5 feet high, 8 to 9 feet long

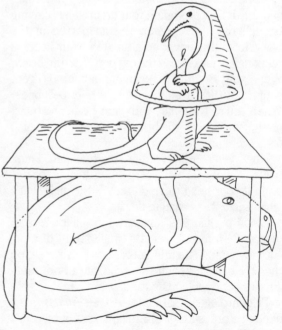

Which dinosaur was as tall as your little sister? Which would fit inside your television set? *Deinonychus* would probably fit nicely in your bed, but watch out for its claws! Spend some time at this and you'll find dinosaurs hiding all over your house!

The Smallest Dinosaur. In the late 1970s paleontologist Jose Bonaparte was searching for dinosaur fossils in Patagonia, a wild region in southern Argentina. What he found surprised everyone—a dinosaur skeleton that he could hold in the palm of his hand. Bonaparte called his find *Mussaurus* (mouse lizard), and it is the smallest dinosaur yet found. He thinks that it is a young prosauropod because it was found near two small eggs, but no one is quite sure which type of dinosaur it would have grown up to be.

What a Mouthful!

A dinosaur's size is easy to judge by looking at its fossilized bones. Once paleontologists know an animal's size, the next question they usually ask is: What did it eat? To answer that question, they look at the animal's teeth.

Miscellaneous Meat Eaters. Most people think of dinosaurs as being ferocious meat eaters. Of the seven major dinosaur groups, however, only one of them, the theropods, ate mostly meat. You can tell this immediately by looking at their teeth.

This illustration shows the tooth of a *Tyrannosaurus*, one of the largest theropods. It shows the tooth's actual size. A *Tyrannosaurus* had 60 teeth in its mouth. It must have had an incredible smile!

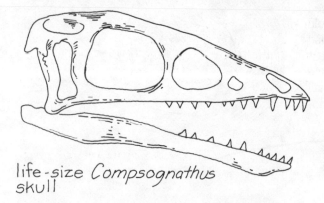

life-size *Compsognathus* skull

Notice how sharp the tooth is and how its edges are rough, just like those on a steak knife. It's perfect for stabbing and slicing through flesh, but not very good for grinding up leaves. It's pretty obvious that *Tyrannosaurus* ate mostly meat.

We should also note that it wasn't only the big dinosaurs that ate meat. *Compsognathus* was only about a foot high. What do you think it ate?

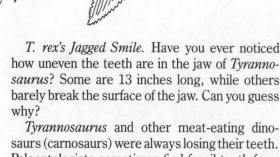

Tyrannosaurus skull

T. rex's Jagged Smile. Have you ever noticed how uneven the teeth are in the jaw of *Tyrannosaurus*? Some are 13 inches long, while others barely break the surface of the jaw. Can you guess why?

Tyrannosaurus and other meat-eating dinosaurs (carnosaurs) were always losing their teeth. Paleontologists sometimes find fossil teeth from meat eaters mixed in among the fossils of a plant eater. As the carnosaur attacked, it would stab the animal with its teeth, and then tear at its flesh.

This takes tremendous force, and teeth were often getting yanked out in the process.

But *Tyrannosaurus* never needed dentures. No matter how many times it lost a tooth, another always grew in to take its place. The smaller teeth in the jaw, then, are the replacement teeth that were still growing when the dinosaur died. Many modern reptiles are able to continually replace teeth. Can you?

Various Vegetarians. As you probably know, plants (in your case, vegetables) can be very hard to digest. An animal has to chew much harder to get nutrients from a plant, while it is much easier to get nutrients from meat.

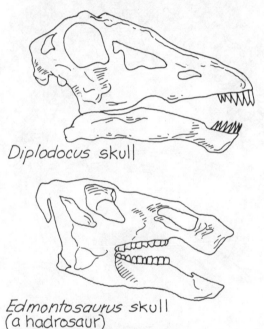

Diplodocus skull

Edmontosaurus skull
(a hadrosaur)

Dinosaurs that ate leaves and plants developed very different kinds of teeth to deal with their diets. The giant sauropod *Diplodocus*, for example, relied on a few small, pencil-shaped teeth for getting its food. A hadrosaur (duck-billed dinosaur), on the other hand, had about 2,000 teeth piled up in its mouth for grinding up tough plants. Though it used only a few dozen teeth at any one time, if one tooth wore out, there was always another to take its place.

When a new tooth appeared in the hadrosaur's mouth, it was pointed, but the constant grinding soon flattened it. By looking at how a hadrosaur's tooth is worn, paleontologists can often tell exactly where the tooth was in the animal's mouth.

The Secret Grinders. Scientists have often wondered how much food a giant *Apatosaurus* ate each day. The answer is obvious. A lot! But how much is a lot? Well, a modern hippopotamus eats about 150 pounds of food a day. And an elephant that weighs about five tons eats up to 400 pounds a day. So *Apatosaurus* must have eaten at least half a ton of plants a day.

It must have eaten continually, all day and all night, to take in that much food. But look at its teeth. They look like little pegs that would give out after one day of such eating. How did it ever chew up such huge amounts of food? It didn't. Not with its teeth, anyway. Look at this illustration. Do you see anything among the bones that looks different?

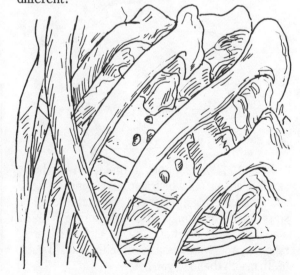

Look closely among the bones and you'll see a number of rounded rocks. Scientists think these might have been the secret of the *Apatosaurus*. You see, modern crocodiles and birds also lack grinding teeth. To make up for them, they swallow stones (called *gastroliths*, or "stomach stones"). These gastroliths come to rest in a special part of the animal's stomach, called the *gizzard*. When food is swallowed, the gizzard's muscular walls churn the stones and food together. The stones crush the food and break it up.

Apatosaurus didn't need teeth to grind its food. It just needed some clippers to nip the fruits and leaves from the trees. Then it swallowed the food whole and let its secret grinders do the hard work. Of course, all this grinding wore down the stones too. When they became small enough, they passed from the gizzard along with the food. That was okay, however; the dinosaurs could always find more. In fact, they were pretty choosy about the stones they swallowed! Can you imagine which kinds of stones make good gastroliths? What qualities would make them better or worse?

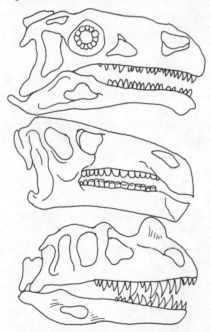

Who Ate What? Look at the teeth in these skulls. Can you tell which animals are meat eaters and which are plant eaters? Look at the teeth of some modern animals. How do a dog's teeth match its food? What about a cat's? A horse's? A rabbit's? And what about yourself? How do your teeth match the food you eat?

Our ancestors developed several different kinds of teeth: canines, or stabbing teeth; incisors for biting off food; and cheek teeth, or molars, for chewing. Can you find the different kinds of teeth in your mouth? How many of each do you have? What do you think humans are designed to eat?

Dilophosaurus

SIZE: 20 feet long
MEANING OF NAME: Two-ridged lizard
TIME PERIOD: Early Jurassic
CLASSIFICATION: Saurischian, theropod, carnosaur, megalosaur
LIFESTYLE: Possibly a scavenger as its jaws aren't well developed
NOTES: An early meat-eating dinosaur
DISCOVERY SITE: Arizona, U.S.A.

Dinosaur Dash

Dinosaurs have always been pictured as dim-witted, giant reptiles that lumbered along in slow motion. But this is the old view. As we've seen, some paleontologists now argue that dinosaurs were warm-blooded, smart animals that scooted around like ostriches.

How fast was fast? In the following activity we'll use math tricks to find out. George Callison is a paleontologist and professor in southern California. He looked at the work other scientists had done to calculate the top speeds of animals and decided to hold a race to see which of the "new" dinosaurs (the ones that were warm-blooded and smart) was fastest. You can conduct your own race to see which was the world's fastest dinosaur. **You will need:**

> **a metric scale that measures to a tenth of a centimeter**
> **a pencil**
> **scratch paper**
> **a calculator is helpful**

Remember, for this activity we are assuming that the dinosaurs were warm-blooded. Many scientists aren't yet convinced that is true. Coming up is the formula you'll need.

The Speed Formula. An animal's top speed depends on the length of its hind legs and the size of its body. To put it simply, longer legs help animals run fast, while larger bodies slow them down. If an animal has both long legs and a large body it will be a so-so runner. If it has short legs and a large body, it will be very slow.

To find out which dinosaur is fastest, measure the length of each animal's leg bones and note its *mass factor* which accounts for its body size. Then use these numbers in the speed formula to calculate each animal's top speed.

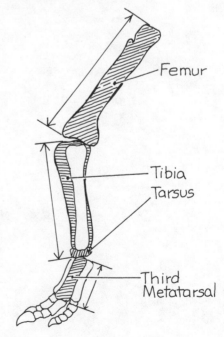

1. Measure the length of each dinosaur's femur; tibia and tarsus; and third metatarsal. Use a metric ruler to measure each bone as accurately as possible and write down these lengths to the nearest tenth of a centimeter.

2. Add the lengths of the bones together. Multiply this by the *scale factor* (20). This gives you each animal's *hind limb length* (HLL).

3. Divide the *hind limb length* by the *mass factor* given for each dinosaur.

4. Multiply this number by 4.132.

5. Subtract 14 from this number. This gives you the animal's top speed in kilometers per hour.

The formula seems complex at first. But if you do one dinosaur at a time and work through the formula a step at a time, you'll get the hang of it.

The Race Is On! First, find out which dinosaur was the fastest in its time period. Then stage a runoff between the winners of the Late Jurassic and Late Cretaceous races to see who's champ. By the way, were dinosaurs getting faster by the Late Cretaceous, or were they slowing down? Late Jurassic: *Allosaurus*, *Camptosaurus*, *Stegosaurus*, and *Apatosaurus*. Late Cretaceous: *Tyrannosaurus*, *Anatosaurus*, *Struthiomimus*, and *Triceratops*.

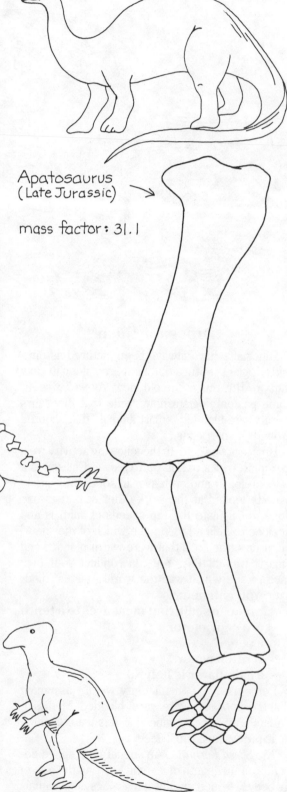

Apatosaurus
(Late Jurassic)

mass factor: 31.1

Stegosaurus
(Late Jurassic)

mass factor: 19.03

Camptosaurus
(Late Jurassic)

mass factor: 5.85

82

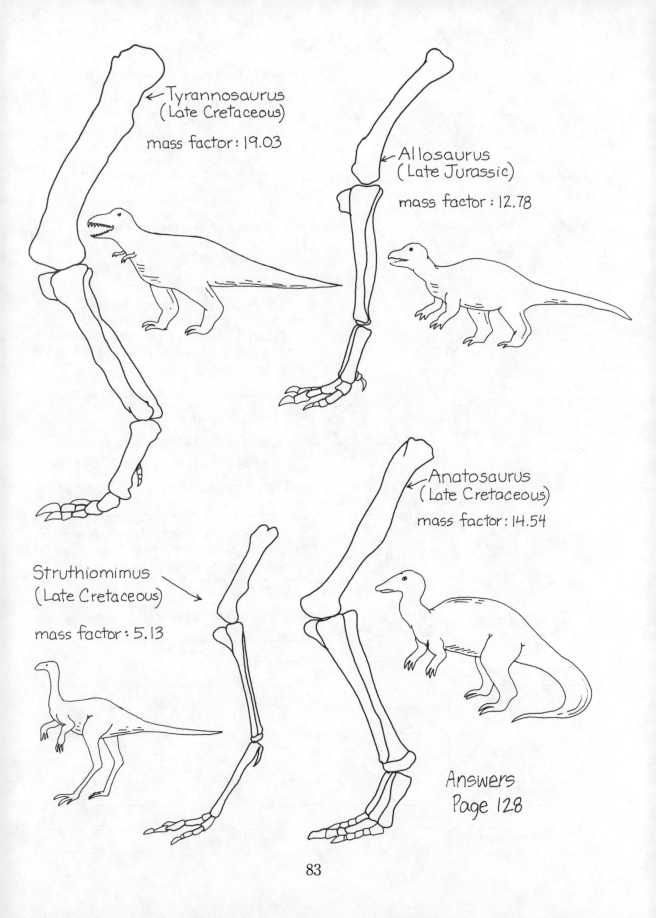

Tyrannosaurus
(Late Cretaceous)

mass factor: 19.03

Allosaurus
(Late Jurassic)

mass factor: 12.78

Anatosaurus
(Late Cretaceous)

mass factor: 14.54

Struthiomimus
(Late Cretaceous)

mass factor: 5.13

Answers
Page 128

Triceratops
(Late Cretaceous)

mass factor: 20.39

Garudamimus

SIZE: 11 to 12 feet long
MEANING OF NAME: Garuda mimic (for a half-bird, half-man creature in Hindu mythology)
TIME PERIOD: Late Cretaceous
CLASSIFICATION: Saurischian, theropod, ornithomimosaur, garudasaurid
LIFESTYLE: Fast-moving, ostrichlike predator
NOTES: May have had a bony crest
DISCOVERY SITE: Mongolia

Note: Scientists throughout the world use the metric scale, and it's good for you to practice using it. If you'd like to see how fast the dinosaurs were in miles per hour, however, multiply its metric speed by 5/8 (.625).

REMEMBER:
These bones are drawn twenty times smaller than the real animals' bones!

Try making a chart like this to record your race results.
(Answers are on page 128.)

DINOSAUR RACE

LATE JURASSIC	HIND LEG LENGTH X	SCALE FACTOR OF 20	MASS FACTOR	TOP SPEED
Allosaurus			12.78	
Camptosaurus			5.85	
Stegosaurus			12.16	
Apatosaurus			31.1	
LATE CRETACEOUS				
Tyrannosaurus			19.03	
Anatosaurus			14.54	
Triceratops			20.39	
Struthiomimus			5.13	

Great Plates

Eureka! You've just found what every paleontologist dreams of: a complete dinosaur skeleton. It's one of the big, plated dinosaurs, *Stegosaurus*, and it looks as if all the bones are together and unbroken. What luck!

It's a huge beast, and it takes several days to uncover and plaster all the fossilized bones. Back at the lab, you begin to reconstruct your dinosaur. Weeks later, you've completed the job, and the bones are laid out in a large room. Here's what they look like:

How strange! From its size you would think that it must have weighed about two tons, but its head is only the size of a large dog's. Those spikes on its tail must have been great defensive weapons, but what are those big bony plates that lie along its spine? And how did they fit on the dinosaur?

What do you think *Stegosaurus* used its plates for? How did they help the dinosaur live? Were they used for protection the way a turtle's shell is? Were they used to attract a mate, as a peacock's feathers do? Or were they for regulating the animal's temperature the way the radiator in your family's car does?

And how were the plates arranged? Did they stick straight up in the air, or did they lie flat? Did they form a single row down the animal's back, or were they staggered in two rows?

Get out a piece of paper and a pencil and do some sketches of how you think the plates might have been arranged on the back of a *Stegosaurus*. Then explain what function you think the plates had and why you arranged them the way you did.

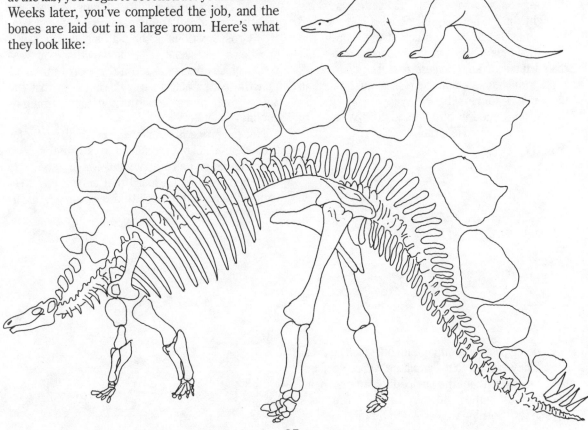

Have you made up your mind? Well, there is no correct answer. Not yet, anyway. But we do seem to be getting closer, and there are a number of paleontologists who are more than willing to tell you their theories.

The first *Stegosaurus* was collected in Colorado and described by Professor O. C. Marsh, one of the most famous early paleontologists. Marsh concluded that the plates were for protection, and he placed them sticking straight up on the animal's back.

For a long time everyone followed Marsh's lead, drawing *Stegosaurus* with its plates sticking straight up. Then some people had second thoughts. "If the plates stuck straight up in the air," they reasoned, "what would keep other animals from attacking *Stegosaurus* from the side?" This group decided that the plates must have lain flat on the animal's back, wrapping around its flanks for added protection. Their version of *Stegosaurus* looked like this:

Recently, a new group got involved in the mystery. They argued that the plates weren't for defense at all. Instead, they helped the animal maintain its body temperature by catching the sun's rays in the morning to warm it and radiating heat off during the hot part of the day to keep it cool. They pointed out that modern elephants use their huge ears to keep cool during the hot African days. In fact, these scientists even did a computer simulation to see which would be the most efficient arrangement for the plates if they were used as temperature regulators. Here's the picture they came up with:

To be most efficient, the plates should be arranged in a single alternating line down the animal's back. Now we have a whole different version of good old *Stegosaurus*. Today, most paleontologists have accepted this latest version of *Stegosaurus*. Cross sections of the plates show that they are heavily vascularized (filled with blood vessels), which gives very strong support to the idea that the plates acted as giant radiators that the animal could pump blood through for warming or cooling.

Not everyone is convinced. Perhaps in the future, new fossil finds will lead to new theories on how the plates were arranged. Maybe someday somebody will find a fossil that solves the mystery. Until then, feel free to draw your *Stegosaurus* any way you like.

Corythosaurus

Lambeosaurus

Tsintaosaurus

Parasaurolophus

Crazy Crests

If you've ever felt self-conscious about the size or shape of your nose, take some consolation from the hadrosaurs. Some of these duck-billed dinosaurs featured outlandish bony head ornaments on the tops of their heads. These crests were hollow and were actually part of the animal's breathing passage.

One hadrosaur, *Parasaurolophus* (rhymes with "parrots for all of us"), had a great arching crest that stuck out more than six feet from its head. Another hadrosaur had a headpiece that resembled the helmets worn by ancient Corinthian soldiers; hence, its name *Corythosaurus*.

The hadrosaurs didn't sprout such elaborate "hood ornaments" just because it made them look cool. Paleontologists have developed a number of theories to explain them. Here are a few for you to consider.

Underwater Diving Gear. There are actually two theories here. The first one is that the crest acted as a snorkel, so the animal could breathe while it was feeding underwater. Only one problem: there's no opening in the top of the crest.

This led to a revised theory. The hollow crest acted as a scuba tank, providing an air reservoir for the animal while it was feeding. This, too, wasn't very logical, as some of the hadrosaurs had very small crests. Besides, there's no evidence that they spent much time cruising around underwater anyway!

Sense of Smell. Hadrosaurs didn't have horns or claws to protect themselves, and they really weren't very fast (they were quite large, up to 20 feet long), so they needed to be able to sense when a predator was approaching.

How? This theory says that they could smell the predator approaching. The crests were connected to the animals' nostrils, and the large surface area inside the crest gave them a very keen sense of smell. The only hitch in this idea is trying to explain why some animals had small crests, or none at all.

Visual Displays. Some of the crests are so flashy, and each type so distinct, that some scientists have concluded they may have been used as visual signals to help the animals recognize others of their own species (the way a soccer or football team wears special colors so the players can recognize one another). The crests may also have been used in courtship rituals or to establish the pecking order within a herd (the male with the largest crest would be the dominant male).

Alarm Systems. The crests may have acted as amplifiers, so the hadrosaurs could produce noisy honking and bellowing to warn other animals of approaching danger or to establish dominance in the herd.

Which theory or theories do you like best? What does your favorite theory tell you about how hadrosaurs lived?

Craft a Crest. You can get a sense of what a crested hadrosaur must have felt like by building a crest that fits on the top of your own head. **You will need:**

> **construction paper (2 sheets)**
> **scissors**
> **tape**
> **pencil**

1. Make a 1-inch band that fits around your head by cutting a 2-inch-wide strip out of the construction paper and folding it in half lengthwise. Measure the strip to fit your head and tape the ends together.

2. Make a second 1-inch strip, as in step one. This band will run over the top of your head, connecting opposite sides of the circular band. Fit it to the top of your head and tape it in place.

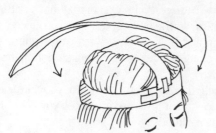

3. Fold the second piece of construction paper in half. Pick your favorite crest and sketch it so that the base begins on the folded edge. Use the patterns shown here, or base your crest on another hadrosaur, but be sure to curve the base as shown and leave at least two tabs.

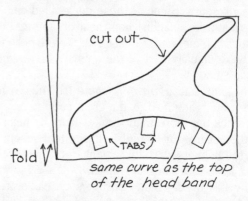

same curve as the top of the head band

4. Measure and mark where the crest tabs meet the headband. Cut slots in the center of the band. Insert crest tabs. Fold them over and tape them in place.

You're done. Now you're a bona fide crested hadrosaur.

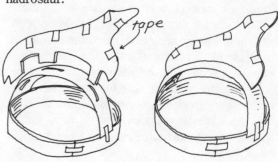

Design Your Own Crests. Hadrosaurs had some convoluted crests, but I bet you can design ones that are even more outrageous. Design a crest that would make you stand out from all the other hadrosaurs. Explain how it functions and how it would help you survive. You can use some of the theories discussed earlier in this activity (snorkel, scuba tank, smelling danger, identification, alarm system), or you can develop your own theory.

Parasaurolophus Tune. Paleontologists will never be able to hear the sounds dinosaurs made, but there is one scientist who thinks he may know what kinds of sounds *Parasaurolophus* could create with its tall, hollow crest. David Weishampel thinks the crest functioned the way a bugle does, producing a deep vibrating sound. For his experiment he built a model of the crest and played various notes into it. The notes A-flat, C, E-flat, and F-sharp were found to make the most resonant tones. If you play a musical instrument, you might try out those notes to get an idea of the range of sounds *Parasaurolophus* could make. Try composing a song that consists solely of those notes.

Mesozoic Mysteries

The "Great Plates" and "Crazy Crests" questions bring up a good point. There are many things that fossils may never tell us. Just as we don't know for sure how *Stegosaurus* plates were arranged, there are a number of other things that we might never know about dinosaurs.

Look at the dinosaur skeleton below. Examine it very closely. Can you tell what color that dinosaur was? Or what kinds of sounds it made? Did it squeak, or did it roar? Was it a good parent? No matter how hard you look, there's no way to say for sure. That's why paleontologists approach these kinds of questions from a different angle—they observe modern animals. Following are two examples.

There's a reason for each animal's color. Think about where each animal lives and how its color would help it survive. Then, next time you're drawing dinosaurs, have some fun with their colors. Give them camouflage patterns (like those the army uses) to help them "disappear" in their environment, or give them flashy colors to help them attract a mate.

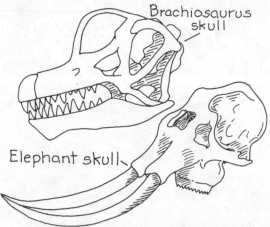

Am I blue? An animal's color is very important. It can help the animal blend into its environment so it won't be seen by other animals. Or it can be used to attract a mate.

Traditionally, dinosaurs have been shown in dull grays and browns. That's because people always thought of them as primitive reptiles. Nobody, however, seemed to give the problem much thought because no one had any direct evidence.

Today, paleontologists are thinking about dinosaurs in different terms, and they're looking at the color patterns of modern animals for clues about how dinosaurs were colored. If dinosaurs were related to birds, could they have been brightly colored the way some birds are? Or maybe *Deinonychus* and some of the other hunters were striped as modern tigers are.

Next time you visit the zoo, be sure to note the animals' colors and think about how they help them. (If you can't get to a zoo, you can look at a good book that has color photographs of animals.) Which animals tend to have brighter colors, large ones or small ones? Why is the polar bear white? How does a lion's coloring help it catch food? Why do zebras have stripes? Why do newborn fawns have white spots on their backs?

Brachiosaurus Proboscis. There's one other thing that doesn't usually show up in the fossil record—the soft flesh of an animal's body. Paleontologists can reconstruct a dinosaur's muscles by examining the places where the muscles attached to the bones. But the soft fleshy parts that hang from the body, such as an earlobe or an elephant's trunk, disappear completely.

That brings up an interesting question. Could any of the dinosaurs have had a trunk like an elephant's? Look at the two skulls above. One belongs to an elephant and the other to *Brachiosaurus*. Notice that both of the skulls have large, high nostril holes. This similarity has led some paleontologists to draw a new version of *Brachiosaurus*.

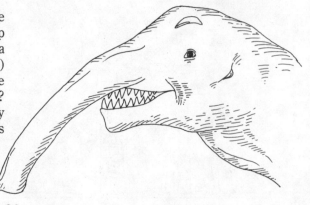

90

CHAPTER

5

BREATHING LIFE INTO OLD BONES

Dinosaur High Society

Imagine you've stumbled upon a dinosaur nesting colony 80 million years in the past. Ear-shattering noises assault you from all sides. You are surrounded by hundreds of 25-foot-long hadrosaurs who bellow and snort as they tend their young and defend their nests. Overhead, giant pterosaurs soar on the wind.

The colony covers an island in a small lake. For as far as you can see, the island is covered with nests, spaced at 30-foot intervals, as if they were on a giant, unseen checkerboard. Each nest is an elevated mound of sand, scooped out at the top and filled with rotting vegetation, potato-size eggs, and newborn dinosaurs screaming to be fed. You draw back as a mother rushes by, her cheeks full of berries and leaves as she tries to satisfy the hungry hatchlings in her nest.

Suddenly there's a commotion at the far end of the colony as a small egg-eating predator makes a rush for one of the nests. Adults hurry to beat off the offender. This time they succeed. The eggs are saved, though many will be lost before the nesting season is over.

This is the world of *Maiasaura*, a hadrosaur that lived in the Cretaceous period. *Maiasaura* may sound different from most other dinosaur names (you're leaving off the final *s*). That's because it is a feminine name meaning "good mother lizard." This name reflects the animals' highly organized social structure. How do we know so much about the life of *Maiasaura*? Because of a remarkable find made in 1978 on the northern plains of Montana. Here's the story of that find.

The Man Who Walks on Eggshells

Jack Horner has a knack for finding the most amazing fossils. Currently the curator for paleontology at Montana State University's Museum of the Rockies, Horner grew up in Montana and found his first dinosaur fossils there as a seven-year-old. Since that time, he has spent every possible moment scouring the countryside for fossils.

In the summer of 1978, Horner was in search of something special. He wasn't looking for any of the huge dinosaur fossils that are so impressive in museums. He wanted to find small ones. The summer before, he had discovered the first dinosaur egg in the Western Hemisphere, and now he wanted to find the rest of the family—babies, adolescents, and adults. He got what he was looking for even before he reached the field.

Spikeosaurus

SIZE: 40 feet long
MEANING OF NAME: Great spiked lizard
TIME PERIOD: Late Tertiary
CLASSIFICATION: Ornithischian, theropod, quillimimid
LIFESTYLE: Lived in underground colonies; survived extinction of other dinosaurs by burying its head
NOTES: Shot porcupinelike quills at its prey
DISCOVERY SITE: Hawaii, U.S.A.

His big break came when he stopped off at a rock shop in Bynum, Montana. The owner of the shop showed him some fossils and then pulled out a coffee can full of small bones. Horner gasped—baby dinosaurs! The shop owner led him to the site where she had collected the fossils. Horner and his crew started digging. Within a week they had uncovered a bowl-shaped dinosaur nest with about fifteen nestlings. By the end of the summer, they had found an entire hill of nests, eggs, and baby dinosaurs.

Since then, Horner and his crew have discovered more nests. In fact, they've found more than 500 eggs at a knoll now known as Egg Mountain. Most of them belong to *Maiasaura*. With the eggs they found the skeletons of recently hatched animals as well as juveniles and adults. Nearby they've uncovered similar nesting sites of at least three other species of dinosaurs. The most recent discovery came in the summer of 1986, when they found a *Styracosaurus* nesting colony.

What happened to these thriving nurseries? Were they suddenly buried by a volcano or a giant mudslide? No one knows for sure, but the prehistoric disaster gives us a unique chance to see how dinosaurs lived. Following are a few of the conclusions Horner and other scientists have been able to make about the dinosaurs' lifestyle based on their discoveries.

Dinosaurs at Home

Dinosaurs have always been portrayed as bad parents, who just laid their eggs and left them. This was logical because many modern reptiles behave that way. But Horner found nests that contained baby *Maiasaura* skeletons that were nearly three feet long and a foot tall. Those nestlings hadn't just hatched—they were probably several months old.

The wear marks on the babies' teeth showed that they had been chewing on tough plants. From this, Horner concluded that the baby dinosaurs were being cared for by one or both parents, who brought food to the nest much like modern birds. An adult *Maiasaura* skeleton found near the first nest was added evidence for his conclusion.

These finds are surprising because parental care indicates a high degree of intelligence and social organization. By protecting their nests and nurturing their young, these dinosaurs ensured that more babies survived. This gave them an advantage over the animals who abandoned their eggs, and it may be one reason why dinosaurs were so successful.

How You've Grown!

The paleontologists also found an entire growth series—eggs, hatchlings, juveniles, and adults. The find gave them the chance to see how fast dinosaurs grew, an important clue as to whether they were warm-blooded or cold-blooded. (When they are young, warm-blooded animals grow much faster than cold-blooded animals.)

You can follow Horner's investigation by trying this activity. You'll need a pencil and some graph paper. First, Horner calculated the growth rate of *Maiasaura*, which grew to 21 feet. Then he obtained similar data for a warm-blooded animal (an ostrich, which grows to 7 feet) and a cold-blooded animal (an alligator, which grows to 7½ feet). Note that both of these animals are thought to be closely related to dinosaurs.

Use Horner's data to draw a graph that compares the growth rates of these animals. Lay it out something like this:

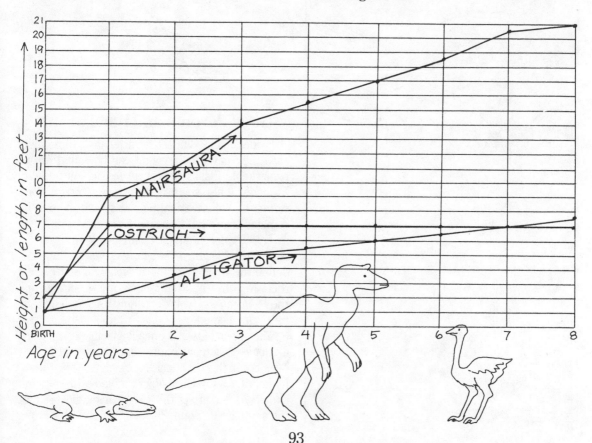

In its first years did *Maiasaura* grow more like an ostrich or an alligator? Is this evidence that it was warm-blooded or cold-blooded?

Try adding your own growth rate to this chart. Your birth certificate will tell you how long you were at birth. If your parents or your doctor have kept track of your height since that time, they should be able to help you assemble enough data to see how humans compare to *Maiasaura*.

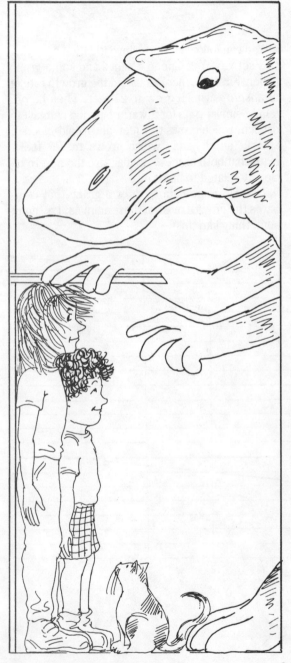

On the Move

The paleontologists working at Egg Mountain have uncovered hundreds of nests in strata laid down at different times. This is evidence that the nesting site was used for a very long time. They also note that very few dinosaur eggs are found just across the border in Canada, though fossils from many of the same species are found there.

From this evidence they have concluded that *Maiasaura* migrated from the lowlands (now in Canada) to the nesting site (now in Montana) year after year to have their young. The fact that these animals migrated over long distances is, once again, evidence that they were warm-blooded because cold-blooded animals aren't capable of such sustained effort.

From these three examples you can see why Jack Horner's discoveries in Montana are shaking up paleontology and changing everyone's ideas about dinosaurs.

Good Parents and Bad Parents

Evidence that dinosaurs varied in the amount of care they gave their young can be found in two remarkable fossils. The first fossil was found in Mongolia when scientists were digging up *Protoceratops*. While excavating a nest, they found the remains of an adult *Protoceratops* mixed with those of *Velociraptor*, a small carnivorous dinosaur. In fact, one of *Velociraptor's* long claws was embedded in the rib cage of the *Protoceratops*. Because the two were found in a nest, it is assumed that the *Protoceratops* was defending its nest when the two animals died.

The second fossil is equally fascinating. It's of a *Coelophysis*, a meat-eating dinosaur found in New Mexico. In this case, paleontologists found the remains of a baby *Coelophysis* mixed with an adult skeleton. Scientists think that this indicates that the adult ate its young.

Egg Zactly

Eggs are among the most fragile fossils. The first dinosaur eggs were found by an American expedition in Mongolia. They belonged to the primitive ceratopsian dinosaur *Protoceratops*. When the eggs were put on display at the 1933 World's Fair in Chicago, the crowds were disappointed—the eggs were so small. Why are dinosaur eggs so small?

Anatomy of an Egg. Dinosaur eggs are hard like bird eggs (not leathery like lizard eggs), and hard eggs can grow only so large because the shells can't be too thick. There are two reasons for this. First, the shell must be thin enough so that oxygen can reach the developing embryo. Second, it must be thin so that the hatchling inside can eventually break out when it is ready. The largest possible egg would be about 24 inches in diameter.

Currently, paleontologists have found eggs from at least nine different dinosaurs. The chart below will give you some information on the different dinosaur eggs that have been found—their size, where they were found, whether or not they were in nests, the number of eggs found in a nest, and the size of the adult dinosaurs.

Grab a chicken egg from your refrigerator and see how it stacks up to these prehistoric eggs. And how does a chicken compare to the adult dinosaurs?

Dinosaur/Adult Length	Egg Size	Egg Shape	Arrangement of Eggs	Nest
*Hypselosaurus** (France), 40 feet	10 inches in diameter	Round	?	?
Hypsilophodonts (Montana), 7 feet	6 inches long	Potato shape	?	Yes; round but smaller than *Maiasaurus*
Maiasaurus (Montana), 25 feet	8 inches long	Grapefruit size, oval	15 to 25, arranged in a circle	Yes; mound 3½ feet high and 6 feet in diameter
*Mussaurus** (Argentina), 10 feet	1 inch long	Smaller than a quarter	5	Yes
Protoceratops (Mongolia), 6 feet	6 to 8 inches long	Potato shape	18 to 30, arranged in a circle	Yes; shallow bowl in sand
*Troödon** (Montana), 8 feet	4 inches long	Oval	Side by side in long rows	No; covered with dirt

*The relationship between the eggs and the adult dinosaurs has not been firmly established in these cases.

95

Egging Them On

Using papier-mâché and party balloons, you can build your own dinosaur eggs. Create a clutch of dinosaur eggs at home, and the next time you're at the beach, you can build a nest for them. First, find a good work space and cover it with newspaper. **You will need:**

newspaper
scissors
assorted balloons (small party balloons—the short ones, not the long ones)
wallpaper paste (or other wheat paste)
water
a bucket for mixing the paste

1. The first task is to find balloons that are the right size for the eggs you want to build. Small party balloons make great *Protoceratops* eggs. You'll need larger ones for *Hypselosaurus* and *Maiasaura* eggs. If you can't find the perfect size, use the balloon that's closest in size. You can always build it up when you add the papier-mâché shell.

2. Cut the newspaper into neat ½-inch-wide strips long enough to wrap once around the balloon. Make long ones to run the length of the egg and shorter ones for the width. If you are making a larger egg, increase the width of the strips a bit.

3. Mix up the paste, using four parts water to one part powder. An egg beater helps to make it smooth.

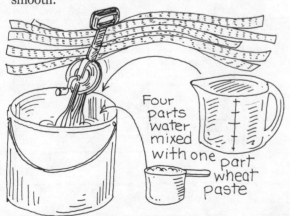

Four parts water mixed with one part wheat paste

4. Dip the newspaper strips into the paste, running them between your fingers to remove the excess liquid, and apply them neatly to the balloon. First build a framework with a few long strips running lengthwise. Then use the short strips to finish the shell.

5. If you are making a large egg, add a second layer, but be sure to let the first one dry completely before beginning the second one.

6. If your egg is lumpy, smooth the shell with fine-grained sandpaper.

One good way to do this activity is to build an egg for each species. Then you can compare the sizes of the different eggs. You can also compare the sizes of the eggs with those of the adult animals. Do bigger animals always have bigger eggs?

Another question to investigate is how large an egg can be. Remember, the shell can't be too thick. Let's limit it to two layers of papier-mâché. Do the shells get weaker as the eggs get larger?

If you plan to build a nest, the dimensions are given on the chart. For a *Maiasaura*, you'll need a pile of sand 3½ feet high and 6 feet in diameter. Then scoop out the top for the eggs. The rotting vegetation the dinosaurs would have used to keep the eggs warm can be left out.

Aww... Why not???

Young Giants. Small eggs present a problem for giant dinosaurs. After all, an adult *Apatosaurus* would have been almost 100,000 times larger than a hatchling from the largest possible egg (24 inches in diameter). Because of this, some scientists are now arguing that *Apatosaurus* and the other large sauropods gave birth to live young. In this case, the newborn would have been about the size of a full-grown pig.

Live birth also ties into another new idea about the sauropods. If you look at old drawings of sauropods, they're always shown wading around in a mucky green pond. Sometimes they're even swimming! Well, that has all changed. Studies have shown that these animals weren't designed for wading around in the mud. Instead, they had hard, firm feet like an elephant's, that were designed for walking long distances on dry ground. Most likely, the sauropods moved around in herds, constantly searching for food.

How does this tie in with live birth? Well, to survive in a migrating herd, a newborn would have to be able to travel almost immediately. A hatchling from a 24-inch egg would not be able to keep up with the adults, but a newborn the size of a pig probably could. From dinosaur trackways we already know that young sauropods did travel with the herd and that they were kept in the middle for protection from predators.

Extinct Possibilities

One of the liveliest debates in paleontology centers on what happened to the dinosaurs. After dominating the earth for 150 million years, why did they become extinct in a relatively short time? Nobody knows the answer yet, but they're working on it. Scientists all over the world are looking for evidence that will explain this mystery. For right now, though, everyone will just have to wait.

Here are the arguments for four of the most popular theories. Read through them and make up your own mind about what happened to the dinosaurs.

First, you need to know a few things about what scientists refer to as the "Cretaceous-Tertiary Extinction Boundary" (it marked the end of the Cretaceous period and the beginning of the Tertiary period). It wasn't just the dinosaurs that disappeared during this time period. Paleontologists estimate that 50 to 65 percent of the plants and animals on the earth disappeared. These included all the large animals on the land, in the air, and in the seas, as well as a number of smaller animals, such as ammonites and squidlike mollusks that lived in the oceans.

Equally puzzling are the kinds of animals that survived—small reptiles, mammals, birds, insects, and fish. The correct extinction theory has to account not only for all the animals that died, it must also explain why certain animals survived.

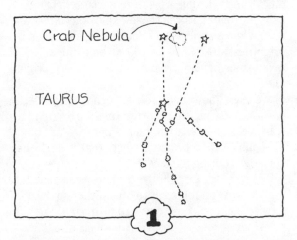

Did It Come from Outer Space?

The Exploding-Supernova Theory. The first extraterrestrial explanation for dinosaur extinction provides a great opportunity to do a little stargazing. If you have binoculars and a star chart, locate the constellation Taurus (the bull). In the Northern Hemisphere, you will find it in the winter sky northwest of Orion, another major constellation.

The tips of the bull's horns in Taurus are formed by two bright stars, Beta Tauri and Zeta Tauri. With your binoculars, or a telescope if you have one, look between these two stars (just above Zeta Tauri) and you'll see a beautiful gaseous formation. This is the Crab Nebula.

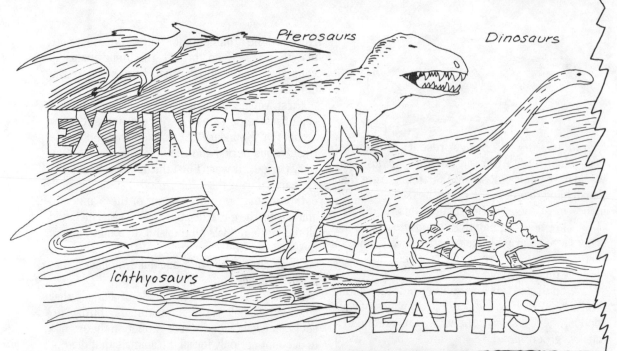

EXTINCTION

Pterosaurs

Dinosaurs

Ichthyosaurs

DEATHS

The Crab Nebula is made up of the gases given off by the explosion of a star much larger than our sun. Astronomers call these explosions *supernovae*. When a supernova explodes, it increases in brightness 10 million to 100 million times, suddenly transforming a faint star into a very bright one.

We even know when this supernova exploded, because the Chinese reported seeing a bright new star in the constellation Taurus in the year 1054. The star was so bright, in fact, that it could be seen even during the day.

Today, more than 900 years later, you can still see the gases. You can't tell from the earth, but they're still exploding outward at more than 600 miles per second. The Crab Nebula is a very distant formation, so only the light of the exploding star reached the earth.

But what would happen if a supernova exploded in a constellation that was much nearer? Would it flood the earth with deadly cosmic rays that would kill many of the animals living on the planet? This is what some scientists think happened to the dinosaurs and other creatures that disappeared 65 million years ago.

People who like this theory, however, need to answer two questions. Why did the cosmic rays kill some animals and not others? And where was the supernova? We haven't yet found the remains of a supernova nearby that may have exploded at that time, so we still need some hard evidence.

②

The Asteroid Theory. The supernova theory suffers from a lack of physical evidence, but another extraterrestrial theory began when scientists found some surprising evidence here on the earth. While testing samples of strata laid down at the end of the Cretaceous period, they found that it contained a high percentage of iridium, a rare element. After the iridium was first discovered in Italy, further tests have been done at sites throughout the world. In every case, the iridium has been found in the same stratum.

Iridium is rare in the earth's crust. Most of it is tied up in the planet's molten core. But in outer space there is a lot more iridium. Asteroids, for example, contain a lot of it. This led scientists to consider an asteroid as the source of the iridium. After much study, they concluded that a giant asteroid, six to nine miles in diameter, must have crashed into the earth.

Early Mammals

Birds

Lizards

Crocodilians

Turtles

Fish

When the asteroid hit, it vaporized and sent up a huge cloud of dust and steam that enveloped the earth. This cloud cut off the sunlight for weeks, or even months. Without sunlight, plants and phytoplankton (tiny animals in the ocean that are the base of the food pyramid there) died. This interrupted the food pyramid so that all the larger plant eaters and meat eaters also died. The only animals that survived were the small scavengers—mammals, lizards, and crocodiles—who could live off the dead animals and plants.

What are the problems with this theory? First, we've never found the huge crater that the asteroid would have created when it hit the earth. Second, fossils found so far seem to indicate that the last dinosaurs died thousands of years before the iridium layer was created. In Montana the last *Tyrannosaurus* fossil found was 10 feet below the iridium layer.

A newer version of this theory takes these objections into account. It says that the extinction didn't happen all at once. Instead it happened during a period of high comet activity that covered

one to three million years. If four or five large comets hit the earth during such a period, it might have caused a series of extinctions over several million years. This matches the fossil record more closely and also explains why no single large crater has been found.

Was It a Home-grown Disaster?

③

The Cooling-Climate Theory. Many paleontologists don't dispute that the iridium layer may be evidence that a large asteroid hit the earth. They don't, however, agree that it caused the extinction of the dinosaurs. Instead, they have concluded that the dinosaurs and other animals were victims of gradual climatic changes that occurred over thousands of years.

Continental drift may have had an important role, for as the continents moved, they created shallow seas that altered ocean currents and wind patterns and caused the climate to cool. Because

99

evergreens were better able to stand the colder winters, woodland plants replaced the lush tropical ferns and trees. In the oceans, the same thing happened as large tropical plankton was replaced by smaller, coldwater varieties.

The scientists who believe the cooling theory note that there are a lot of signs of stress among the dinosaurs during the late Cretaceous. For one thing their eggshells became much thinner during this time. Among modern birds thin-shelled eggs are often a sign of stress.

The number of dinosaur species also dwindled. Paleontologists working in Alberta, Canada, have found that there were 35 species of dinosaurs 73 million years ago, dropping to about 25 species 68 million years ago, and only 6 species 65 million years ago. So the dinosaurs were disappearing long before the asteroid hit.

The weakest point in this theory is that it is difficult to explain the extinction of the marine reptiles. Could a gradual cooling of the water really have affected the plankton?

The Volcano Theory. Some scientists have concluded that volcanoes were responsible for the iridium layer. The late Cretaceous was a period of great tectonic activity—continents were moving into new positions. This activity would have been accompanied by volcanoes and earthquakes. The volcanoes may have blown the iridium from deep within the earth's core into the atmosphere. Such an eruption would also raise a tremendous amount of ash and dust. Winds would carry these particles around the world, enveloping the earth in a cloud. This caused the earth to cool, which interrupted the food chain.

Could volcanic activity really cause such drastic changes in the earth's temperature? Those who back this theory note that when Tambora, a large volcano in Indonesia, exploded in 1815, the ash cloud was so thick that it caused the earth to cool. The next summer was extremely cold, with summer snowfalls and frosts throughout the world. They also argue that old craters indicate that the volcanoes of the late Cretaceous were much larger than Tambora.

You Decide. These are a few possible theories that scientists are investigating. Each one has strengths and weaknesses. Which theory sounds best to you? Can you think of other reasons to explain why dinosaurs became extinct? This is one of the most controversial topics in paleontology right now. Many scientists are working on the problem. As they announce their results, you will probably see a number of articles in newspapers and magazines. Read these articles to see if the latest data support your theory.

Return of the Dinosauroid

A few years ago, Canadian paleontologist Dale Russell asked an interesting question: "If the dinosaurs hadn't become extinct at the end of the Cretaceous, how might they have evolved?"

To answer the question, Russell took one of the smartest dinosaurs, *Stenonychosaurus*, and tried to guess how it might have developed through time. These animals were fast runners who had long, grasping fingers for catching their prey. Russell assumed that *Stenonychosaurus* would gradually become more intelligent until it could capture food by outwitting other animals. As its hands developed, it might even have learned to make crude tools. He called his creature a *dinosauroid*.

Does the dinosauroid sound like any other kind of animal you can think of? What might have happened had dinosaurs such as *Stenonychosaurus* survived? Would mammals (like you) still have been able to dominate the earth if they had had to compete with these advanced dinosaurs?

Chasmosaurus

SIZE: 17 feet long
MEANING OF NAME: Ravine lizard
TIME PERIOD: Late Cretaceous
CLASSIFICATION: Ornithischian, ceratopsian, ceratopsid
LIFESTYLE: Browsed in herds on tough plants; adults may have formed defensive circles to protect the young from meat eaters
NOTES: Its huge frill had large holes in the bone to reduce its weight
DISCOVERY SITE: Alberta, Canada

Whose Extinction?

Nearly 98 percent of the animal species that have lived on the earth are now extinct. In fact, there is evidence of extinctions throughout the earth's history. You're probably just more aware of the extinction at the end of the Cretaceous period because it affected the dinosaurs.

Right now, some people say we are living through a period of mass extinctions. Almost 50 species of mammals, birds, and fish have disappeared in the last hundred years, and this rate is sure to increase. Already, more than 100 other species are near extinction.

There are probably animals in your area that are threatened. In California, for example, the last wild condor was recently captured and put into a zoo. Scientists hope that it will be safe there and that it will breed with other condors that were captured earlier. Some day, once the population of condors has increased, they hope to reintroduce them into their natural homes.

Find out about other animals that are in danger of extinction and what people are doing to save them. You can look for this information in the library, or you might try contacting wildlife conservation groups.

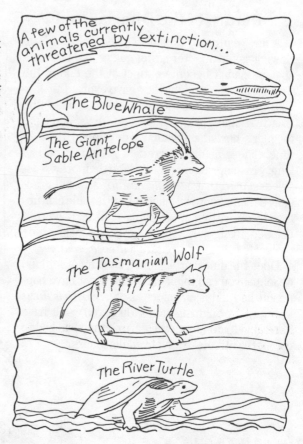

A few of the animals currently threatened by extinction...

The Blue Whale

The Giant Sable Antelope

The Tasmanian Wolf

The River Turtle

6

KEEPING THE DINOSAURS
ALIVE

As mentioned in the beginning of this book, dinosaurs bring out the best in people. They spur our interest in exploring new things and new worlds. It's important that we keep this creative spirit alive. The activities in this chapter will give you some ideas of ways to nurture the dinosaur lover in everyone.

Rewriting the Book on Dinosaurs

Remember, the story of the dinosaurs, as we know it today, is our own invention, based on the hard work and investigations of hundreds of people. It's a story that is being rewritten all the time. In fact, 40 percent of all the dinosaur species identified have been discovered since the late 1960s. And there are probably hundreds more

waiting to be described. Right now, paleontologists all over the world are hard at work uncovering new fossils or studying old ones. The result of all this effort is a constant flow of information that changes our ideas about dinosaurs.

Because the public is fascinated with dinosaurs, many of these stories end up in newspapers. You can keep tabs on the developing story of the dinosaurs by keeping a scrapbook of newspaper and magazine articles that document new discoveries and theories.

If you live in a small town, dinosaur articles may be scarce in your local newspaper, so ask your relatives and friends to save articles for you. You might also look through magazines and newspapers at the library. But don't cut out these articles; photocopy them.

You'll soon have a surprising number of articles. In a recent six-month period, newspaper articles have appeared on:

1. The discovery of the first dinosaur fossils from Antarctica.

2. The discovery of *Seismosaurus* in New Mexico, a dinosaur that appears to be longer than *Diplodocus*.

3. The discovery of *Baryonyx* in England, a peculiar fish-eating dinosaur.

4. A revised version of *Stegosaurus* that gives it a single row of alternating plates.

5. The discovery in Montana of *Avaceratops*, a new miniature ceratopsian dinosaur.

Stories like these are continually appearing. Stay alert, and maybe someday you'll have an idea that helps rewrite the book on the dinosaurs.

Elect a State Fossil

Republicans and Democrats aren't the only old fossils hanging around the state capitols these days. All over the country, dinosaurs and other prehistoric beasts are finally being recognized by state legislators, who are honoring them as state fossils. Who do you think is responsible for this movement? It's one of the country's newest lobbying groups—school kids.

Currently, we know of 13 states that have state fossils. They include:

California, saber-toothed cat;
Colorado, *Stegosaurus*;
Georgia, shark's teeth;
Louisiana, palm wood;
Maryland, *Ecthora quadricostata*;
Massachusetts, dinosaur track;
Montana, *Maiasaura*;
Nebraska, mammoth;
Nevada, ichthyosaur;
New Mexico, *Coelophysis*;
North Dakota, teredo wood;
Ohio, trilobite;
and Wyoming, *Knightia* (fossil fish).

If your state hasn't chosen a fossil yet, why not take up the cause? It's not easy. You'll have to do a lot of research and a lot of letter writing. You'll need to get a lot of friends to help you. But most of all you'll need a whole lot of patience and determination.

Here's the story of one class of Colorado kids who worked for almost two years to have *Stegosaurus* named their state fossil.

THE STEGGY STORY

The idea started in January 1980, when the fourth-grade class at McElwain Elementary School in Thornton, Colorado, was studying the early history of their state. One day their teacher, Ruth Sawdo, read in a United States Geological Survey magazine that Utah had named *Allosaurus* its state fossil. (Later, it turned out that the legislature had never made it official.) When she told her students about Utah's state fossil, they began to wonder if Colorado had honored a dinosaur in a similar way.

When the students found out that Colorado didn't have a state fossil, they decided to take action. First, they had to decide which dinosaur best represented the state. They wrote to paleontologists around the state asking them to name their favorite Colorado dinosaur. When all the votes were in, they decided that *Stegosaurus* should be the official state fossil. After all, the first *Stegosaurus* skeleton was discovered near Morrison, Colorado, in 1877.

Next, the students had to interest the state legislators in their plan. Fortunately, the mother of one of the students was Polly Baca-Barragan, a state senator, who promised to introduce their bill honoring *Stegosaurus*.

True to her promise, Baca-Barragan introduced the bill on January 27, 1981. When the Senate Affairs Committee considered the bill, three students from McElwain School went to the capitol to make a formal presentation. They must have been pretty convincing, because the committee passed the bill unanimously.

Next, the bill would be considered by the entire senate. The students knew they would need lots of support, so they began a letter-writing campaign. They wrote to students at other schools, museum directors, newspapers, radio and television stations, and to every member of the senate. In all, they wrote more than 2,000 letters!

The students campaigned in other ways too. They printed *Stegosaurus* T-shirts. Everyone in the class got one, and they even presented one to the governor. They also invited a professional lobbyist to their school to give them ideas for their campaign. At her suggestion, they circulated petitions at a local shopping mall, gathering more than 1,000 signatures in support of honoring *Stegosaurus*.

Despite all their efforts, the bill didn't become a law that year. Though it passed in the senate, it didn't even come up for a vote in the house. In Colorado, a bill must be passed by both houses of the legislature before the governor can make it a law. "Steggy," as the stu-

dents had come to call their adopted dinosaur, would have to wait another year.

The dinosaur probably wasn't too disappointed. After all, it had already waited 150 million years for the honor. When the next legislative session opened, the students were ready.

They produced a slide show on the dinosaur. They put Steggy into a diorama at Colorado Mining Days. They created *Stegosaurus* murals and statues. Most impressive of all, they invited all the state legislators and the governor to lunch in the school cafeteria. After finishing off the meal with Steggy-shaped cookies, the students presented the case for their dinosaur.

Once again the students went to the capitol to testify. But once again, the legislative session ended without considering the bill. Things looked bleak.

Then came a big surprise. The governor had been impressed by the students' hard work. One day he called to tell them that he wanted to come to McElwain to make an announcement. On April 28, 1982, Governor Richard Lamm appeared at the school in front of TV cameras and newspaper reporters to sign an executive order proclaiming *Stegosaurus* the official state fossil. The McElwain students were overjoyed. *Stegosaurus* had finally achieved the recognition it deserved.

The students also had another reason to celebrate. After all, they had learned a lot about how laws are made and how citizens can affect those laws. They also learned how important it is to keep working for something you believe in, even when things look bleak.

Start Your Own State Fossil Campaign. If your state doesn't yet have a state fossil, get busy! Here are a few tips for starting a campaign.

1. Be dedicated. Organize a good group of creative friends who want to work really hard—the more people the better.

2. Be knowledgeable. Learn about the fossils that have been found in your state. Which types are they? Why are they significant? If you can't find this information in your school or city library, you might try a natural history museum or science center, local rock shops or gem and mineral clubs, geology or paleontology teachers at local colleges, or the State Department of Geology. Invite a geologist or paleontologist to speak to your group about the fossils in your state.

3. Be selective. Write letters to geologists and paleontologists asking them to help you select your state fossil. Choose the fossil that best represents your state. Develop a list of arguments to support your choice.

4. Be prepared. Learn how bills become laws in your state, and develop a plan for helping your bill pass the hurdles. Once your bill is introduced in the legislature, you might be asked to testify in its support. Have your arguments ready.

5. Be adventurous. Ask your state senator or representative to introduce your bill. (He or she may enjoy some good publicity.) Present your arguments in a well-organized, persuasive manner. If possible, make your presentation in person.

6. Be everywhere. Begin a letter-writing campaign—contact everyone you can think of who could help your bill become law. These may include state legislators; the governor and other state officials; mayors, council members, and other city officials; paleontologists, geologists, and teachers; newspapers and television and radio stations; and teachers and students at other schools.

Ask all these people to write letters to their state representatives in support of your idea. Also, circulate petitions to gather signatures of people who want your state to have an official fossil. Present the petitions to the legislature or governor.

7. Be persistent. Passing a law takes time. Many people may tell you that you're wasting their time, that they have more important things to do. Keep in mind that educating people about your state's geologic history and the amazing prehistoric animals that once lived there is a *very* important goal.

8. Be creative. To be a good lobbyist, you have to be able to attract media attention and influence legislators to support your cause. The McElwain students were very creative in their campaign—presenting the governor with a *Stegosaurus* T-shirt and inviting legislators to a dinosaur lunch.

Organize activities such as those to attract attention to your campaign (and invite television and newspaper reporters to your events too). Good luck!

Beaten to the Punch? If your state already has a state fossil, there's still a lot of work you can do. Do some research to find out which fossil has been honored and why it was chosen. Put together a report on your state's prehistory and use the information to get your friends interested in paleontology.

Dinosaur Ditties

Rhyming in dinosaurese is tricky (the names and scientific words are so long), but it can also be fun, especially when your poem actually tells people about the dinosaurs. Check out all the dinosaur names on page 42, learn about the dinosaurs named, and write a rhyme that tells people about them. Here are a couple of examples:

Poor *Tenontosaurus*,
his story could never bore us.
For he lived in constant fear
of being eaten it's clear
by a carnivore known as *Deinonychus*.

A *Tyrannosaurus* from the Cretaceous
was acting quite bodacious.
"I won't go extinct,"
he said with a wink,
"but my appetite sure is voracious!"

The Creature with Two Brains. Bert L. Taylor, a newspaper columnist, was a master at rhyming in dinosaurese. When he heard that *Stegosaurus* had an enlarged hip nerve that controlled its back legs and tail, he decided to have some fun with the idea of a creature with "two brains." His poem appeared first in the *Chicago Tribune* in 1912. It's probably the most famous dinosaur ditty of all.

Today, we know that the *Stegosaurus* didn't really have two brains, but the poem is still fun, and it reminds us of what special animals dinosaurs really were.

Deinocheirus

SIZE: A mystery
MEANING OF NAME: Terrible hand
TIME PERIOD: Late Cretaceous
CLASSIFICATION: Saurischian, theropod, ornithomimid (?)
LIFESTYLE: A meat eater (that's all we can be sure of)
NOTES: Known only from its arm bones; each arm was 8½ feet long, with three huge claws
DISCOVERY SITE: Mongolia

THE DINOSAUR

by Bert Leston Taylor

Behold the mighty dinosaur,
Famous in prehistoric lore,
Not only for his power and strength
But for his intellectual length.
You will observe by these remains
The creature had two sets of brains—
One in the head (the usual place),
The other at his spinal base,
Thus he could reason *a priori**
As well as *a posteriori.***
No problem bothered him a bit
He made both head and tail of it.
So wise was he, so wise and solemn,
Each thought filled just a spinal column.
If one brain found the pressure strong
It passed a few ideas along.
If something slipped his forward mind
'Twas rescued by the one behind.
And if in error he was caught
He had a saving afterthought.
As he thought twice before he spoke
He had no judgment to revoke.
Thus he could think without congestion
Upon both sides of every question.

*A Latin word meaning "before the fact."
**A Latin word meaning "after the fact."

Dinosaur Hunting in the Wild West

The first paleontologists that explored the American West in the last half of the 1800s were fascinating men. They braved incredible dangers and harsh conditions to pursue their science. The stories of their adventures fill many books. Here are a few of the best.

One of the first paleontologists to explore the West and see its tremendous potential for studying paleontology and geology was Dr. Ferdinand Hayden. A passionate scientist, Hayden's behavior puzzled the Native American tribes that watched him. Here's one legend that has grown out of one of Hayden's early expeditions.

THE MAN WHO PICKS UP STONES RUNNING

It was 1853 in the Dakota Badlands. The Sioux who lived in the area had carefully watched a small group of U.S. soldiers traveling across their land. Of particular interest to them was a small bearded man who didn't travel with the others. Instead, he ran from one hill to another tapping the bare ground with his pick, then stuffing something into a bag he carried over his shoulder. Without pausing, he'd rush on to the next big hill.

The Sioux watched him for some time and discussed his peculiar behavior among themselves. Finally, their curiosity overcame them. They captured him and seized his precious canvas bag. When they shook out the bag's contents, however, all that fell out were rocks.

Finally, they understood that the man was crazy! They carefully refilled his bag and let him go on his way. From then on they referred to him with a Sioux name that meant "He Who Picks Up Stones Running" and allowed him to move freely about their land.

110

MAGIC TOOTH

All the early paleontologists fascinated the Native Americans, and most of them received a nickname. Professor Marsh's Pawnee scouts, for example, referred to Marsh as Heap Whoa Man because he was constantly stopping his horse to inspect an interesting rock or bone. His interruptions made it difficult to get anywhere.

Professor E. D. Cope also had a nickname, but he wasn't named for his travel habits. Here's the story.

The year was 1876, the same year that the Sioux under Sitting Bull had defeated Custer at the Little Big Horn. Cope had been warned by the army that it was too dangerous to collect that summer, but he had ignored the warnings.

One day Cope's crew found themselves camped across the river from a large Crow camp. The Crow were friendly and were simply gathering for their annual buffalo hunt. As a gesture of friendship Cope invited six Crow chiefs to his camp for breakfast. Cope's assistant, Charles Sternberg, relates the story. "Just before breakfast, as was his custom, Cope was washing his set of false teeth in a basin of water, when a party of six stalwart chieftains strode up in single file. . . . Quickly slipping his teeth into his mouth, Cope advanced to greet his guests, who shouted as one man, "Do it again! Do it again!" He repeated the performance for them again and again much to their mystification.

"After they had tried to pull out their own and each other's teeth, and had failed, they settled down to breakfast."

From that day on, Cope's nickname among the Crow was Magic Tooth.

What a Way to Make a Living. When you look at a dinosaur skeleton in a museum, it's hard to imagine the many difficulties the paleontologist who collected the fossils faced. This story might give you an idea of what I mean. It was taken from Arthur Lakes's field notes. Lakes worked for Professor Marsh at a famous site in Como Bluff, Wyoming. Note that the first entry is dated during the middle of a cold Wyoming winter.

"Feb 5th 1880. Collecting at this season is under many difficulties. At the bottom of a narrow pit 30 feet deep into which drift snow keeps blowing and fingers benumbed with cold from thermo between 20 and 30 below zero and snow often blowing blinding down and covering up a bone as fast as it is unearthed."

A letter Lakes wrote later that year, when he was uncovering the first *Stegosaurus* skeleton, shows that things soon got even tougher. "All these bones have been got out with considerable difficulty owing to the spring bursting out and covering them with a lot of water. I had to bale with one hand and dig out a bone as I got a glimpse of it with the other, sitting at the time in a frog pond. More like fishing for eels than digging for bones. Meanwhile snowing and freezing hard so what with water mud and slush it is no wonder if some small pieces are missing."

Fortunately for us, collectors such as Lakes kept working under these harsh conditions. Thanks to their efforts, people can study complete fossil skeletons in museums all over the world.

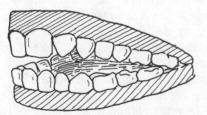

Dinosaur Vacation

Would your family enjoy a Dinosaur Vacation? You can start planning your trip right now! There are museums, science centers, dinosaur fossil sites, even one zoo, that feature public dinosaur exhibits. In some places you can see complete skeletons. Others feature full-size models. In a few places you can watch paleontologists uncover fossils.

Here's a short list of places in the United States and Canada that feature permanent dinosaur exhibits. It's not a complete list, but it will give you a start. Write letters to the places you would like to visit. Ask them when they're open, what you can see when you visit, and if they're planning any special events or field trips for families.

Many science centers also have temporary exhibits that feature moving dinosaur models. Some museums even offer dinosaur classes, field trips, and tours. The Lawrence Hall of Science at the University of California at Berkeley, for example, offers an annual DinoTrek that takes families to dinosaur quarries and museums throughout the western United States. The Oregon Museum of Science and Industry in Portland takes older kids, 13 to 18 years old, on fossil digs at its Hancock Field Station Mammal Quarry.

UNITED STATES

Arizona

Museum of Northern Arizona
P.O. Box 720
Flagstaff, AZ 86001

Petrified Forest National Park
Arizona 86028

California

California Academy of Sciences
Golden Gate Park
San Francisco, CA 94118

Los Angeles County Museum of Natural History
900 Exposition Boulevard
Los Angeles, CA 90007

Museum of Paleontology
University of California
Berkeley, CA 94720

Colorado

Denver Museum of Natural History
Colorado and Montview Boulevards
Denver, CO 80205

Dinosaur Valley Museum
Fourth and Main Streets
Grand Junction, CO 81502

Colorado (continued)

Trail Through Time
Near Grand Junction, CO
Phone (303) 243–DINO

Connecticut

Dinosaur State Park
West Street
Rocky Hill, CT 06067

Peabody Museum of Natural History
Yale University
New Haven, CT 06520

District of Columbia

National Museum of Natural History
Smithsonian Institution
Washington, DC 20560

Illinois

Field Museum of Natural History
Roosevelt Road at Lake Shore Drive
Chicago, IL 60605

Kansas

Museum of Natural History
University of Kansas
Lawrence, KS 66045

Massachusetts

Museum of Comparative Zoology
Harvard University
Cambridge, MA 02138

Michigan

University of Michigan
Alexander Ruthven Museums
1109 Geddes Avenue
Ann Arbor, MI 48109

Montana

Museum of the Rockies
Montana State University
Bozeman, MT 59715

New Mexico

Ghost Ranch
Ruth Hall Paleontology Room
Abiquiu, NM 87510

New Mexico Museum of Natural History
1801 Mountain Road NW
Albuquerque, NM 87104

New York

American Museum of Natural History
Central Park West/79th Street
New York, NY 10024

Pennsylvania

Academy of Natural Sciences
Logan Square   19th and The Parkway
Philadelphia, Pennsylvania 19103

Carnegie Museum of Natural History
4400 Forbes Avenue
Pittsburgh, PA 15213

Texas

Dinosaur Valley State Park
P.O. Box 396
Glen Rose, TX 76043

Fort Worth Museum of Science
1501 Montgomery Street
Fort Worth, TX 76107

Utah

Dinoasur National Monument
P.O. Box 128
Jensen, UT 84035

Prehistoric Museum and Cleveland-Lloyd Dinosaur
Quarry
College of Eastern Utah
Price, UT 84501

Earth Sciences Museum
Brigham Young University
Provo, UT 84602

Utah Field House of Natural History State Park and
Dinosaur Gardens
235 East Main Street
Vernal, UT 84078

Utah Museum of Natural History
University of Utah
Salt Lake City, UT 84112

Wyoming

Geological Museum
University of Wyoming
P.O. Box 3254
Laramie, WY 82071

CANADA

Alberta

Calgary Zoological Gardens
Prehistoric Park
Calgary, Alberta T2M 4R8

Museum of Paleontology Field Station
Dinosaur Provincial Park
P.O. Box 60
Patricia, Alberta T0J 2K0

Provincial Museum of Alberta
12845 102 Avenue
Edmonton, Alberta T5N 0M6

Tyrrell Museum of Paleontology
P.O. Box 7500
Drumheller, Alberta T0J 0Y0

Ontario

National Museum of Natural Sciences
Ottawa, Ontario KA1 0M8

Royal Ontario Museum
Toronto, Ontario M5S 2C6

CHAPTER

7

KIDS MAKE GREAT PALEONTOLOGISTS

"Kids are a lot sharper than adults when it comes to fossils." This comment, made by a paleontologist, appeared in a newspaper story that told how Dylan Zack, who was nine years old at the time, had discovered a fossilized whale skeleton on the beach while his family was vacationing in Santa Cruz, California.

Throughout the history of paleontology, kids like Dylan have proven to be great fossil finders. Pliny Moody, a Massachusetts farm boy, was 12 in 1802 when he uncovered the first dinosaur footprints found in North America. Another famous young fossil collector was Mary Anning. Here is her story.

Lightning Strikes in Lyme Regis

Mary Anning lived in Lyme Regis, a popular English beach resort. Mary's father had always made extra money for the family by selling fossils he found in the cliffs along the beach. When he died in 1810, even though Mary was not yet 12 years old, she set up a fossil shop to support the family.

Later that year, Mary made her first major find, collecting a large ichthyosaur skull and pelvis that eventually ended up in the British Museum of Natural History. Mary's discovery was the first ichthyosaur to be recognized as a new species. Ten years later, she found the world's first plesiosaur, and in 1828 she found Britain's first pterosaur.

As word spread of Mary's special abilities, prominent scientists would arrange to vacation in Lyme Regis so that they could have the privilege of fossil hunting with her. When she died, the city installed a stained-glass window dedicated to her memory in the local church. You can still see it there today.

A number of legends have developed over the years to explain Mary's great success as a fossil hunter. One of the most intriguing is that when she was less than a year old she and her nurse were struck by lightning. The nurse died, but Mary survived and was transformed. Before the accident she had been an unexceptional child, but afterward she became "lively and intelligent, and grew up so."

It's a little more difficult these days to find the "first" of anything, but kids are still carrying on in the fossil-hunting tradition of Mary Anning and Pliny Moody. Here are the stories of two young fossil hunters.

Dinosaurs in Her Backyard

How would you like to have dinosaur fossils in your backyard? Kristie Redding does. She lives on a wheat farm in northcentral Montana, smack dab in the middle of one of the world's best dinosaur fossil-hunting grounds.

Kristie was introduced to fossils in the summer of 1980 when a paleontology crew from the University of California at Berkeley began prospecting on her farm. They found the fossils they were looking for, and since that time they have returned every summer. Each time they visit they teach Kristie a little more about how to look for fossils and how to identify her finds. One summer they let her help uncover and prepare a four-foot-long femur (a legbone) from a duck-billed dinosaur. After she helped take the femur out of the ground, Kristie donated it to the Earth Science Museum in Loma, Montana, where it's on public display.

Even when the paleontologists aren't around, Kristie finds fossils. Sometimes she finds them near her house, but she also goes on fossil-hunting trips with her folks. In 1986, when she was 12, she did a science project, "My Backyard," in which she explained the geography of her area and the different kinds of fossils she has found there. She won first place in the local science fair and took second place in the state competition.

Kristie keeps a large drawer full of fossils in her home. Whenever anyone visits, she shows them her collection. Someday she hopes to find a *Triceratops* tooth for her collection. Where will she look for this rare fossil? In her backyard, of course!

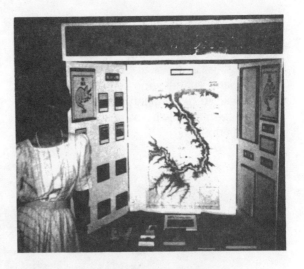

Ammonites and Dinosaur Extinction

Nicole Itano hasn't found any dinosaur fossils yet, but she has become an expert at finding fossils of ammonites (sea animals with coillike shells) and other small animals that lived during the time the dinosaurs were around. Nicole became interested in fossils when she found a broken baculite (another sea creature) that was part of an old rock collection.

With her family, she has hunted for fossils in Texas ("I found some big baculites there") and in California (where she found fossil scallop shells), as well as near her home in Boulder, Colorado. She has also found fossil shark teeth.

Ammonites interest Nicole because they're so unique looking and also because they are from creatures that died out at the same time that the dinosaurs disappeared. "All the ammonites we've found near our home are from the Cretaceous,"

Nicole explains, "because that's when Boulder was part of a seabed. Ammonites disappeared at the same extinction boundary as the dinosaurs, but some small animals survived—the nautiluses and the clams continued to evolve. I don't know what happened to the ammonites. I don't know how a meteorite could have affected them unless it landed in the sea."

Nicole doesn't know if she'll make a career out of paleontology, but she does like it as a hobby. She has already used fossils for her school science projects. One year she compared fossil shells with modern shells. Another year she used ammonites to investigate a mass extinction that took place 100 million years ago in the early Cretaceous period.

Kids at Heart

To be a good paleontologist, it helps to get hooked early on dinosaurs. Many of the good paleontologists working in the field today got their start by finding fossils when they were young. Jack Horner, who has discovered huge dinosaur nesting sites in Montana, is working in almost the same area where he found his first fossils—the rear end of a duck-billed dinosaur—when he was seven.

Arnie Lewis, the chief preparator at the Smithsonian Institution (he supervised the mounting of all the spectacular skeletons in the new Dinosaur Hall), is another example. He got his start in 1933 when a crew from the Carnegie Museum opened a quarry on his family's ranch near Leota, Utah.

Arnie was seven at the time, and he loved to watch the crew dig fossils out of the quarry. When the paleontologists returned in 1935, they invited him to be their "camp boy." Every year after that, they would stop by the farm to pick up Arnie, and he'd spend the summer prospecting for fossils with them. As Arnie remembers, "It got me away from the farming, which was great!"

The area around Leota is rich in fossils from the late Eocene period, and the paleontologists were finding large mammals such as *Titanotheres*. Arnie was nine when he found his first major fossil, the large skull of an *Amynodon*, an Eocene rhinoceros. This was the start of a career that would take him first to the Carnegie Museum, then to Harvard, and finally to the Smithsonian. During that time he has traveled to South America, Africa, and throughout North America looking for fossils.

Arnie's story is fairly typical, it's just that he got started in the business quite a while back. Dan Chaney, another paleontologist at the Smithsonian, also got started when he was young. He found his first fossil in New Mexico in 1957 when he was in the fifth grade. His family had been looking at property near Los Alamos when Dan, his brother, and his sister got bored and wandered off. They found a hill with a small cliff on one side and started jumping off it into a pile of sand.

During one jump Dan noticed a funny rock sticking out of the cliff, so he grabbed a stick and started digging. It turned out to be a camel metapodial (footbone). That got him interested, and he started collecting fossils.

After a number of years, Dan sent some pictures of the fossils he had found to the American Museum to be identified. This led to an exchange of letters and, eventually, to an invitation to join a museum crew working in western Nebraska. Dan worked with these paleontologists every summer while he was in high school.

Today, Dan's interest in fossils has turned into a career that has taken him on expeditions all over the western United States, as well as to Pakistan and Antarctica. At the Smithsonian he's preparing specimens for an exhibit entitled "The Changing Earth." Next time you're in Washington, D.C., be sure to stop by to see his work.

Don't Forget Your Dinosaur Hunting License

The people who live in Uintah County in northeastern Utah live in the heart of one of the best dinosaur bone yards in the world. Because it includes Dinosaur National Monument and a number of other famous dinosaur sites, some people call it Dinosaur Land.

To encourage people to visit Uintah County, the local travel board has developed a whimsical dinosaur hunting license based on Utah's deer hunting license. "Issued by Authority of the U.S. Reptile Control Commission" and signed by "Commissioner Al E. Oop," the license spells out a number of rules for capturing dinosaurs and other prehistoric creatures. For example, you can take only one *Tyrannosaurus* (adult male)," while for pterodactyls the limit is "four only (without young)." The back side of the license lists all the different things you can do when you visit Dinosaur Land.

To get your own dinosaur hunting license, write to DINAH, Vernal, UT 84078. The license is free, but they ask that you include a legal-size, stamped, self-addressed envelope with your letter. Happy hunting!

Welcome to Dinosaur Land
Vernal, Utah

"Dinah" the Dinosaur invites you to [stay a while] ity in a land of breathtaking beaut[y ...] located on U.S. Highway 40 betwe[en ...] Also located on the new Canyonla[nds ...] lands National Park and Yellowstor[e ...] to do, see and enjoy!

DINOSAUR NATURAL HISTORY MUSEUM: Utah's [...] geology and a 500 million year fossil record are gra[...] (Diplodocus) replica and a second life-like dinosaur gro[...] one of the Country's finest fluorescent mineral collectio[...] 9:00 a.m. - 6:00 p.m. in winter. Admission 50¢, 12 to 65.

DINOSAUR GARDENS: 14 life-size, authentically scul[...] natural setting. Admission included above.

FLAMING GORGE DAM: This Upper Colorado River Pr[...] the Vernal-Manila Highway (Utah 44). Flaming Gorge [...] creates a lake stretching 91 miles through the Uintas, ne[...] are numerous campsites, several boating marinas, and m[...] of visitors. You'll thrill at the scenery and the FUN... wh[...]

DINOSAUR NATIONAL MONUMENT QUARRY AR[EA] history of the dinosaur. From this world famous dinosau[r ...] east of Vernal, it is 3 miles from the headquarters to the [...] facilities for camping and picnicking.

DINOSAUR NATIONAL MONUMENT CANYON ARE[A] National Monument at Dinosaur, Colorado. The trip to [...] affords a magnificent view of the 2500 foot canyon of the [...] the "Steamboat Rock." Take your camera.

BOAT TRIPS: Explore the beauties of the Green and Y[...] canyons. A new adventurous experience for young and o[...] rafts.

"REMEMBER THE MAINE" PARK: A beautiful scenic [...] picnic tables, fireplace, lights, water, and rest rooms.

PETROGLYPHS: Prehistoric Indian cliff murals. These [...] animals, etc. familiar to the people of long ago.

RED CANYON OVERLOOK: Red Canyon is located 6 r[...] (Utah 44). A new visitor lookout point with fine exhibits [...]

HUNTING AND FISHING: (In Season) Deer, Elk, Pheas[ant ...] lake fishing, including pack trips into lakes of High Uint[as ...]

STEINAKER STATE PARK: 5 miles north of Vernal. T[...] camping.

SPECIAL EVENTS: Two big rodeos, late June and late [...] Tournament, Indian Ceremonial Dances, boat trips on th[...]

VERNAL PUBLIC SWIMMING POOL: Take a refreshing [...] pool for toddlers, clean, spacious bath house.

DINALAND GOLF COURSE: This nine-hole course with i[...] with the famous "Split Mountain" for a background, will [...]

UINTAH COUNTY DAUGHTERS OF UTAH PIONEE[RS] settlings of this area. Located on 2nd South and 5th We[st ...] Day. Admission free.

FACILITIES: Churches: most prominent Christian faiths [...] several swimming pools, good cafes, dining rooms.

For detailed information on these and many oth[er ...] information center at the Utah Natural History M[useum ...] DINAH, Vernal, Utah 84078

DINOSAUR HUNTING LICENSE

S P E C I A L   P E R M I T
*No. 181 - U022

ISSUED TO:

NAME _____

ADDRESS _____

CITY _____ STATE _____ ZIP _____

ISSUED BY AUTHORITY
U.S. REPTILE CONTROL COMMISSION
Restricted to Uintah County, Utah, Only

This license entitles holder to hunt for, pursue, shoot, kill and remove from that area known as Dinosaur Control Area of Uintah County, Utah, which is in the vicinity of Dinosaur National Monument the following types of reptilian wild game:

A. TYRANNOSAURUS REX - 1 Only (adult male)

B. DIPLODOCUS GIGANTICUS - 1 Only (either sex) and not less than 5000 lbs. live weight

C. STEGOSAURS - 2 Only (males) any size

D. PTERODACTYL - 4 Only (without young)

The holder of this license agrees to remove all such game, legally bagged by him under the proper restriction, properly preserved and in sanitary condition within 5 days of time of reptiles' death, and further agrees to have said game inspected by the Utah Game Warden before removal.

Signed _____

ISSUED BY AL E. OUP
Deputy Lizard Warden, Vernal, Utah

ALTERATIONS ERASURES OR OBLITERATIONS VOID THIS CERTIFICATE

*SPEAK the number. "I eight one, you ought to too."

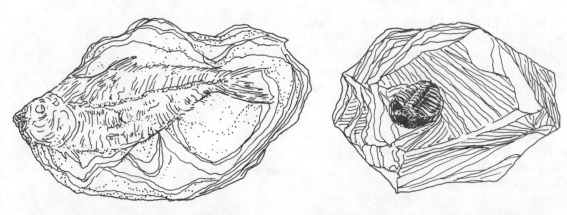

Find Your Own Fossils

Whether you realize it or not, there are probably areas rich in fossils near your home. If you're really lucky, they may be dinosaur fossils. Even where I live in California, within an hour's drive of downtown San Francisco, there are remains of prehistoric hippos, camels, and giant ground sloths.

Even if you're looking *just* for fossil clams, though (something that doesn't seem too exciting at first), the work becomes interesting when you realize that the clams are probably millions of years old. With this in mind, even the smallest find is fascinating. If you're interested in trying your luck at uncovering fossils, here are a few tips to get you started.

Find Out What You're Looking For and Where to Look. Before you grab your pick and strike off for the nearest hill, there's research to be done. Start asking around about fossil sites. You might try your science teacher, local rock collectors, or rock shops. (Look under *Lapidary* in the yellow pages of your phone book.)

Other sources of information might include natural history books in your community or school library, the geology department of a local college, or the geological survey for your state. When you contact these people, explain that you are interested in learning about paleontology and that you want to get experience looking for fossils.

If there are no fossil localities near your home, find out if there are any within driving distance. Then start getting your favorite grown-up interested in a paleontology field trip. Also, a fossil-hunting trip is a great activity for school or community groups.

Remember, hunting for fossils is a skill. The first few times you go, you may not find anything. Be patient. Besides, the hunt itself is half the fun. If you keep working at it, and if you keep developing your ability to know where to look and what to look for, you'll soon develop a knack for finding fossils.

123

Where to Look. Good paleontologists are always looking for "exposures." These are places where geologic formations can be easily seen at the surface and where there is little grass or vegetation covering the ground. Good exposures can often be found in eroded cliffs near streams, rivers, lakes, or ocean beaches; in the sides of roads or railways that cut into hillsides; or at construction sites, quarries, or gravel pits where the earth has been cut away.

Wherever you decide to look for fossils, be sure to get permission from the owner of the land and your parents before you set out. Also, let people know where you are going and when you will be back. That way, if you aren't back on time, they know where to look for you.

Geology Maps. When a paleontologist is considering prospecting in a new area, she or he will first get a good geology map. These colorful maps show which geologic formations are exposed in an area. By finding out which formations are exposed, the paleontologist can zero in on areas that might produce good fossils.

If you'd like to get a geology map that includes your area, contact your state's geological survey. Also, the American Association of Petroleum Geologists has compiled good geology maps that cover the entire United States. For ordering and price information write to American Association of Petroleum Geologists, P.O. Box 979, Tulsa, OK 74101.

124

What to Take. Once you've found a place to look for fossils, the next question is what tools you should bring. Uncovering fossils can be hard work, and you'll need some digging tools. These might include a geologist's hammer or pick for rough work and an ice pick for close-up work. Also, bring a one-inch or two-inch paintbrush for dusting away dirt as you uncover your find. Toilet paper or newspaper is valuable for wrapping small specimens for the trip home.

A notebook and pen for taking field notes are essential items because the most important piece of information about a fossil is where it came from. You may even want to bring a camera to take pictures of the site. Paleontologists often do that.

When prospecting, be sure to take something to eat and drink, and check the weather forecast to make sure your clothes are right for that day's weather.

Locating Specimens. Seeing fossils in the ground is an art that can only be developed with practice. If you go hunting with an experienced person, he or she can help you. If you are on your own, look for shapes and textures that differ from the surrounding rocks. With time, you will learn to differentiate easily between fossils and rocks.

If you come upon a large bone, it is probably best to let a professional paleontologist uncover it for you, as it may be very fragile. As a paleontologist uncovers a fossil, he or she hardens it with a shellac mixture or Glyptol. And before taking it out of the ground, it must be wrapped in paper and a plaster cast to protect it on the trip to the laboratory.

If you find a large specimen, carefully write down a description of its size, shape, and the precise location in your field notebook. Photograph the specimen, as well as its locality, with enough background detail and landmarks to ensure that it can easily be found again. Cover the fossil back up with dirt to protect it from the weather, and mark its location on a map.

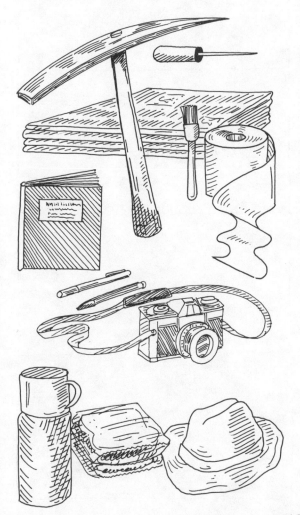

Field Notes. Get into the habit of taking notes whenever you prospect for fossils. Your field notes should include your name and the date of the trip, the site, and a description of what you found and where you found it. The location should include a description of its relationship to local geography as well as in which geological stratum it was found. Use maps whenever needed to describe the site.

Just like a real detective, it's important to write down everything you can think of that might be useful later. You'd be surprised how much you forget as time goes by, and sometimes a small detail will jog your memory about the location of a fossil.

Getting Started. Hunting fossils is an art. At first you might not find anything, but with patience and experience you will continually get better at it. For more information on planning a fossil-collecting field trip, read *The Fossil Collector's Handbook* by James Reid Macdonald. This practical field guide is the best. Not only does it tell you what to take on a field trip, what to look for when you arrive, and how to uncover and prepare the fossils after you find them, it also includes ideas for setting up a fossil lab in your home and a state-by-state guide to fossil sites.

126

The End (or the Beginning?)

This is the end of the book. But if you're hooked on dinosaurs, it's really just the beginning. Dinosaurs still have a lot to teach us. Dinosaur hunters search the ends of the earth looking for fossils; they use their imagination and logic to travel through time; they look at today's world in new ways to see what it reveals about these ancient beasts. Many people have spent their lives unraveling dinosaur mysteries. Fortunately, there are still plenty of mysteries left for the rest of us. Happy hunting!

Answers for page 53

Turtle shell

Hadrosaur teeth

KEY
Hadrosaur — tibia, teeth
Carnosaur — teeth
Turtle — shell, leg bone
Fish — scales, vertebrae
Crocodile — teeth, armor
Lizard — jaws
Salamander — jaws
— vertebrae

Hadrosaur tibia

1, 2, 3, 4, 5 — Salamander vertebrae

Salamander jaws

Fish scales

Fish vertebrae

Carnosaur tooth

Lizard jaws

Fish scales
Fish vertebrae
Turtle leg

Carnosaur teeth

Turtle shell

Crocodile scales

Crocodile tooth

Lizard jaws

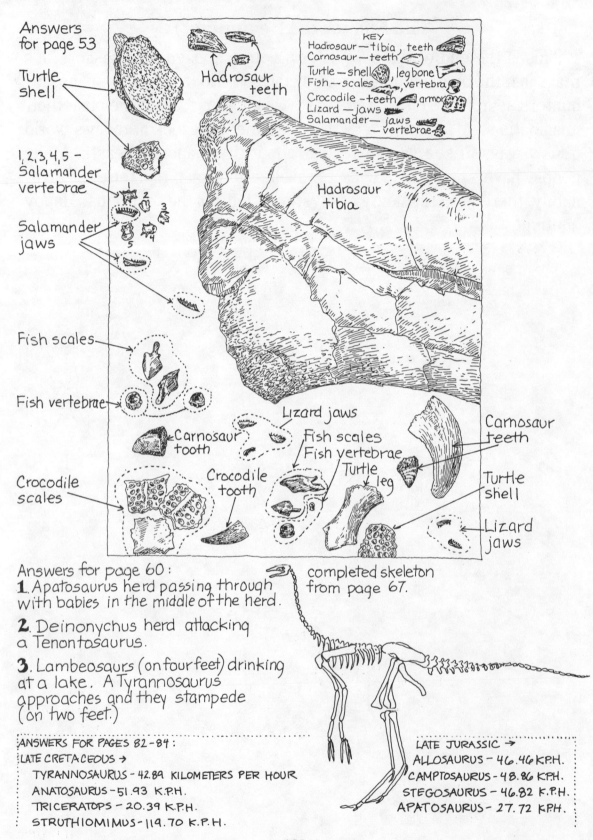

Answers for page 60 :

1. Apatosaurus herd passing through with babies in the middle of the herd.

2. Deinonychus herd attacking a Tenontosaurus.

3. Lambeosaurs (on four feet) drinking at a lake. A Tyrannosaurus approaches and they stampede (on two feet.)

completed skeleton from page 67.

ANSWERS FOR PAGES 82-84 :
LATE CRETACEOUS →
   TYRANNOSAURUS - 42.89 KILOMETERS PER HOUR
   ANATOSAURUS - 51.93 K.P.H.
   TRICERATOPS - 20.39 K.P.H.
   STRUTHIOMIMUS - 119.70 K.P.H.

LATE JURASSIC →
   ALLOSAURUS - 46.46 K.P.H.
   CAMPTOSAURUS - 48.86 K.P.H.
   STEGOSAURUS - 46.82 K.P.H.
   APATOSAURUS - 27.72 K.P.H.

9087